DATING
season
Books 5 & 6

paige press

DATING *Season*
Books 5 & 6

LAURELIN PAIGE
AND KAYTI MCGEE

Copyright © 2021 by Laurelin Paige & Kayti McGee

All rights reserved.

No part of this book may be reproduced in any form or by any electronic or mechanical means, including information storage and retrieval systems, without written permission from the author, except for the use of brief quotations in a book review.

Paige Press, LLC
Leander, Texas

Ebook ISBN: 9978-1-953520-88-3

Paperback ISBN: 978-1-953520-89-0

Content Editing: Paula Dawn at Lilypad Lit

CopyEditing: Erica Russikoff at Erica Edits

Proofing: Michele Ficht, Kimberly Ruiz

Cover: Laurelin Paige

SPRING FEVER

EPISODE 5

It's time for spring cleaning, but I'm not ready to toss Logan yet...

Out with the old, in with the new... a new me, that is. Now that Charlotte's married, I, too, have decided to be mature. So Logan isn't Austin--that's okay. Better than okay. That's what I'd wanted all along, someone just as kind and loving and--okay, smoking hot--as my roommate. But a kind, loving, smoking hot someone who likes me back.

Logan has basically been all my dreams come true.

If I could stop stressing about work for five whole

minutes to appreciate it, I'm sure I would be really happy. Thank God I have Austin to keep me grounded. Literally, because he makes me garden with him now. And maybe it's just the stress talking, but it kind of seems like he wants to put down roots too. How come no one told me maturity would be this complicated?

ONE

VALENTINE'S DAY is meant to *celebrate* love, not end it. Somehow, I managed to get through the ending I needed, only to discover this? Austin's announcement that he and Lucy broke up rides a merry-go-round in my head, whirling endlessly, making me dizzy.

I'm having a *Princess Bride* moment. When people say they're shocked, I don't think it means what they think it means. What's happening to my body isn't your ordinary surprise pumped up a notch or two. I'm talking about true immobilization of limbs and brain function.

Timing is everything, and sadly, Dawn has none. "Chloeeeeee, wait for meeee," she slurs, rushing toward me in the parking lot where I stand, slack-jawed, staring at Austin. "Could you give me a ride home?" She teeter-totters to a stop, unaware she's preventing me from asking Austin why Lucy ended things.

"If it's too much trouble...I'll just sleep here." She waves her hand vaguely at the parking lot.

"No, no," I pull myself together and say. "Of course it's not too much trouble." And I'd do it even if it were. I almost killed a man once, and that's the sort of thing that haunts you. Leaving Dawn in a parking lot in February would definitely be tantamount to murder.

"Thank you. Where's your hawt drummer?" She turns to Austin before I can answer. "Your girlfriend caught the bouquet. Aw. Invite me to your wedding."

Technically, Lucy stole it, but that's not important. What's important is Austin's strained smile is painful to see.

"She's not my girlfriend anymore," he says. "We broke up."

Dawn gasps. "Oh gosh. How awkward. I'm so sorry," she says, disappointing me when instead of asking what happened, she launches into a rambling story about how if she'd only worn different heels, maybe she'd have caught the bouquet. "Of course, maybe catching it is a bad thing? Phew, glad I didn't catch it. Not that I have a boyfriend, but if I did, we might not be together anymore. And then I'd be sad."

She scrapes her red nails down the lapel of his tux, nearly causing me to rethink leaving her in the lot. "Are you sad?"

"I'm good," he says.

"You are," she says. "I can tell. Speaking of telling, don't tell Charlotte I had too much to drink."

After we pinky swear, Austin is a gracious gentleman at foiling her attempts to "help him forget" as we load her drunken body into my car, buckle her in, and shut the door.

"Do you need me to follow you to her house? And then I can follow you home."

An uncomfortable silence lingers in the brisk air before I answer. "Oh, that's okay. I, uh, was on my way to Logan's from here."

"Ah." He steps closer, but not close enough in the dim lighting of the parking lot for me to read what's going on in his mind. "Chloe...I..."

Dawn knocks on the passenger window with a succession of sharp raps. "Ready when you are."

"Just one minute," I say, and turn back to Austin. "Do you want to talk about what happened?"

Dawn opens the door and sticks her head out. "Set a timer on my phone. Forty-five seconds left and counting."

"I'll be right there," I say as she counts down how much time remains.

Austin chuckles. "You should get going. We can talk later."

"I can drop her off and come home—"

"No," he interjects, "I need to run by the restaurant and check out some things."

Call it intuition, but I don't believe that. "Are you okay?"

"Yeah," he says, but I'm not convinced. "I'll see you tomorrow."

He walks away, and I do the only thing I can think of to make him feel better.

"Austin," I call out as he opens the door of his car. "Did you know the moon is actually shaped like a lemon and not round?"

His crooked grin makes me grin. "I did not know that. That's why I like you so much."

Of course he waits for me to leave the lot before he drives away. I blow out a breath. They broke up. There was a time I dreamed of this very thing happening. But now that it's happened, I don't know what to think. Chances are they'll get back together, so it's best I not think about it at all.

But thinking about it is all I do as I drop off Dawn at her apartment and get her inside where she hooks me up with a change of clothes so I don't have to do a walk of shame a second time.

I think about it more as I drive to Logan's and

park in the driveway. Then I don't want to think about it any longer and tuck it away so I can regroup and focus on having a good time with Logan...and the band?

"Hey, C," Liam greets me as I enter the kitchen with Logan. "Want to join us for poker?"

"They cheat," Belinda says from her spot at the island. "Fair warning."

I scoot on the stool next to her. "I've never played so I'll just stay over here."

Logan kisses the top of my head and joins the guys at the table, and I put my focus on having a great night. Sort of.

"How's Lucy?" Belinda asks. "Liam said she nearly killed you catching the bouquet. Guess there will be a second wedding soon."

"I don't know," I say, squirming in my seat. "She and Austin broke up."

Her brows raise. "The last time I saw her, she said they were moving in together. Huh. That's a shocker. Maybe when she thought about what catching the bouquet truly meant, she freaked out."

Belinda tells me a cute story about how she panicked and ended things with Liam when he proposed to her. Right now, I kind of wish she were boring, so I could tune her out, but I listen with rapt attention as she tells me it's normal to get cold feet with serious commitment and more than likely they'll get back together.

"So does that mean he's staying at your place?" Logan asks.

"Yeah," I answer.

"Does that mean you're not moving? Because my offer still stands."

I have no answer and luckily, I don't need one because Will throws down a royal flush. Logan asks to see what he's hiding in his pants.

"You just want to see my dick again."

Their continued banter makes me laugh. This is how my life would be if I lived with Logan all the time. And it's...nice. Not like *my* home, but nice. Huh. When did I start thinking of the place I share with Austin as home? It is, though. More than just the place I live. It's where my heart is. Where I live, love, laugh. Where throw pillows get their inspiration.

Once everyone leaves, Logan takes my hand and brings me to the couch. His pillows don't say anything, but they *are* extremely comfortable. "So, I feel you should consider an important perk of living here."

"Oh, really? And what perk is that?"

He picks up a remote from the coffee table and music filters into the room from the surround sound system. "A striptease. One of many perks you'd get as my roommate."

A slow, sensual song filters from the surround sound as he eases up his T-shirt, revealing luscious abs, inch by etched inch.

The black cotton sails across the room, giving me an unobstructed view of rippling muscles beneath golden skin.

"I'll need to see more," I say, mesmerized by the sway of his hips.

He nudges my knees apart, stepping between them to lower his zipper and discard the remainder of his clothes in a slow tease. His cock points at me, and my nipples point back. As the music wraps us in a sensual cocoon, as he not only strips himself, he undresses me too.

"Not only will you get stripteases"—he leans down and scoops me into his arms—"you'll get treats."

"I do love treats," I say as he stalks toward the kitchen, depositing me on the cool granite island.

"I do too. Especially when they're eaten off of a beautiful woman." He opens the fridge and withdraws a tall can of Reddi-wip. Extra creamy. The kind Austin never buys because he creates his own dessert topping from scratch. Also, extra creamy. In the roommate wars, I'd have to give the point to

Logan, because Austin never preferred to eat his off of me.

Logan: 1

Austin: 0

Okay, maybe half a point for Austin's homemade cream because it's so delicious. Once, I ate the whole bowl.

Logan: 1

Austin: 1/2

"I've wanted to taste your tits all night." Logan squirts a mound of whipped cream on my breast and sucks it into his mouth, grazing my nipple with his teeth. I grip the counter's edge. Playing with food is a new sexual experience, and it's definitely upping the chances of me accepting his roommate offer.

"Mm," he murmurs as he applies the same decadent attention to my other breast.

"That feels so good," I pant out.

"We'd have dessert nights," he tempts. "I'd make a sundae on your pussy." He squirts a fresh trail across my collarbone, lapping it up with his tongue, sucking a path up my neck and nipping my lobe. "Then I'll fuck you in the shower."

I moan as he slips his hand between my legs, exploring my seam. "That's a damn good sales pitch."

"You're so wet," he marvels, peering down at his fingers pumping inside me.

Finally, he kisses me, and I wrap my palm around his hardness, stroking. When his skilled hand has me edging toward an orgasm, he lifts me and stalks toward the bathroom, straight into the shower.

Our hungry kiss continues as he twists on the water, and a steamy spray fills the tiled enclosure. Logan wins another point when he sinks to his knees and glides his tongue inside me, gripping my ass to bring me closer to his face. Although, if I'm being fair, Austin has this cool shower bench that makes it really easy for me to sit and shave my legs. If not for that, the leg now over Logan's shoulder as he devours me might not be as smooth. But I'd say Logan wins again when he rises and spins me around, reaching around the shower curtain to pluck a condom from a drawer before entering me from behind.

"Oh God," I cry out as my hands slap against the tiled wall, bracing myself for his deep strokes.

Logan: 2

Austin: 1 (I really enjoy that shower bench, so another half point.)

"Damn, Chloe," he says. "I could come just watching you. No one has ever made me think about that."

I deduct half a point from Logan's total because now I'm thinking about how many people Logan's had sex with in this shower. I'm sure he's had his fair share, given the amount of females hanging around the band at their gigs.

Those thoughts swirl out of my head and down the drain when he slams into me and adds a twist of his hips, sending tingles all the way to my fingertips. My orgasm hits me so hard, my knees buckle.

Logan grunts and pumps faster, until he releases on a sexy moan. Shower sex is a definite plus, in the perk department. So is watching him wash himself after the deed. And watching him watch me as I dry my hair.

Once we're in bed, Logan traces circles on my shoulder. "How's Mae'd doing?"

Great sex and pillow talk? Unf. I fill him in on my business and how it's booming with website orders and tell him about my new project with Something Borrowed.

"You'll be taking over the pottery world soon," he says in a drowsy voice. "My back deck would be a perfect place for your pottery wheel."

We briefly talk about me possibly moving in, but avoid talking about whether I'd be moving in as a "roomie" or a "girlfriend." Oddly, I'm okay that we haven't said that word. It's nice to have no labels. My heavy eyelids can barely stay open when he mentions it would be awesome to have someone there to water his plants when he's on tours.

Hm. I'm a little fussed that it might be the former, but too tired to analyze it.

In the past, I probably would've found a reason I should agree and then made excuses why I agreed. But, I realize, I don't know if I want to water his plants. And that's okay.

So I say I'd rather not decide yet, and I'm going to see if Austin will sign a month-to-month lease while we figure out our Next Steps In Life.

Winner: Chloe

TWO

MESSY BREAKUPS ARE MORE likely to cause depression than other tragic moments in your life. Believe it or not, even more so than death. It worries me. I needed help, and the internet never fails to provide. So as Logan made pancakes this morning, I searched the web for tips on the best ways to help Austin through his split with Lucy, because this isn't an ordinary breakup like the ones I've experienced.

I mean, he's been part of a "we" for over a year. Now, he's just an "I," and that's a tremendous change. According to the internet gurus, it's possible he could even suffer an identity crisis, so it's best I am prepared for anything and everything.

You'd think since I've had more than my fair share of breakups that it would be smooth sailing for me to navigate Austin through the tumultuous sea of heartbreak. But that's not the case. Unlike my failed relationships, Austin and Lucy were pretty darn serious, so I can't relate to the depth of what he's probably feeling now that they are over. Even if what he's experiencing is foreign to me, I can still support him with all the expert knowledge I gained this morning.

I even made an anonymous post on FriendsOfFriends and the consensus is that I need to ease his burden by distracting him from thinking about it and also that I am still in love with him. Which I am *not*.

I *closured*.

My plan involves just being there for him with no judgments. That's what he did for me, and I'm going to return the favor and be the best friend I can be for as long as he needs me. It's important for me to approach things with compassion and no matter what he tells me, be careful with my words because what if they get back together?

When I arrive home and walk in the door, Austin is unleashing his emotions on the hardwood floor, Swiffering at a rapid pace across the living room. The music notes on his arms dance as his biceps flex from the amount of muscle he's putting into it. Other than that, he looks normal. You'd never guess he's experiencing emotional trauma. He's not moping nor schlubbing around in wrinkled pajamas, like I tend to do when I'm upset with life. He's dressed in worn jeans and a black T-shirt, hair gleaming in the sunlight filtering through the open blinds on the windows.

"Hey," I say, in the gentle tone I used on Coco, because I'm not sure what mood to expect.

Anger, sadness, and confusion are all possibilities.

He glances up and hits me with a devastating smile. "Hey, roomie."

I smile, but I don't know how to respond. Over this past year, I've learned it's not beneficial to me to hold things inside and just hope it works out in my best interest. In a glorious sign I've matured, I blurt out, "*Are* we roomies? Logan asked me to move in, but with you and Lucy…"

"Wait. Hold up." He props his duster against the wall. "He asked you to move in?"

I perch on the couch's arm. "Yeah. Last night after the wedding."

"You barely know him." He runs a hand through his hair, rumpling the dark tresses. "Why would he ask you to move in so soon?"

Lucy's comments about "big brother" blare in my head. Will he ever realize I'm a grown woman? "I don't know, because I needed somewhere to live?"

Is it really that odd? Not everyone lives by society's acceptable timetable. Granny Mae only knew my grandfather for a week before they got hitched. What's normal to one person isn't necessarily normal to another, but now Austin's got me thinking that— what if it really *is* all about watering his plants?

"You have somewhere to live," he says. "You know you can stay here if you want. Do you not *want* to stay?"

This is not going how I planned. It's not supposed to be about me. I'm here to help him through his suffering and find out what happened. "Well, I didn't have a place twenty-four hours ago when he asked me. He was just being nice."

"Are you going to move in with him?"

A crease forms between his brows, and even though I want to smooth it out by assuring him, the new and mature me isn't rushing into decisions anymore. I should give it more time to decide where I'll end up living permanently, wait until he's stronger and less vulnerable. After all, what happens if I decide to stay and then Lucy comes back into the picture? The only thing worse than not having Austin as a roommate would be having them both.

"Maybe we should do it month-to-month while we figure out, you know...whatever?" I think it's probably impolite to just say he needs to figure out *his* life before we commit to anything long-term.

He sighs, heavily. "I agree we have to figure out

the...whatever. So we're on the same, you know, page."

I nod, wondering if we'll ever be on the same page. Usually I feel like I'm in a different book than everyone else. Regardless, it feels wrong to abandon him right now so I say, "I'm definitely in for staying. For a while. If month-to-month works for you, then sign me up."

"Month-to-month works for me. If that's what you want." His dark eyes look so forlorn that my chest aches. "I can give you time to figure things out. I'm not going anywhere."

Ugh. Speaking from experience, after a breakup, as much as I wanted to burrow in my bed and dwell on my faults, it's helpful to have friends who refuse to let you wallow in despair. I need to practice being a good friend and keeping him busy.

"Great." I stand. He's already cleaned, and I'm not hungry, what else can I assign him? "Hey, maybe we can plant that garden you were wanting."

That perks him up, and his eyes brighten. "Yeah, I'd like that. I've been putting it off for too long."

I'm good at this being a Good Friend supportive thing. I should lean into this and take the moral support further. "Should we talk? No pressure, though. Whenever you're ready."

"Yes. We should definitely talk." He turns and heads toward the kitchen. "I'll make us breakfast."

I follow behind him. "Well, Logan made pancakes before I left, so we can just talk. You don't have to cook me anything."

He stops mid-stride. "He cooks?"

I nod and scoot past him. "Yeah. You two actually have a lot in common."

Still in the entryway, he crosses his arms, eyes narrowed. "What flavor?"

"Blueberry." They were delicious, picture perfect, light and fluffy with crisp edges. But I feel Austin's too fragile to handle that information, so I keep it to myself.

"Whipped cream on top?"

"Um, no. Just syrup."

He shakes his head. "That's not the kind you like or how you like them. Did he bother to ask how you liked them?"

Ugh. I can't tell him there was no whipped topping because he ate it off of me before shower sex. Or that it turns out I didn't think I liked blueberry pancakes because I'd never had real blueberry pancakes, just the sad fast-food variety that I was today years old when I discovered aren't even made with real blueberries. I'm sure he's feeling sensitive right now after being dumped, and needs a self-esteem boost, so I say, "Yeah, but you know, I can always find room for one of your delicious omelettes."

That works. The rigid squareness leaves his shoulders, and he moves to the refrigerator. I take a seat at the dinette table, ready to be a good listener. I'm dying to get some answers about their split, but it's not a good idea to pressure him into discussing it before he's ready. While I wait for him to spill the tea, he pulls out a carton of eggs. Then a block of cheese, but still silence. Then a baggie of spinach...a stick of butter...a skillet...a spatula...and a mixing bowl. No tea. He focuses on cracking eggs and whisking them into oblivion, and I realize it's time to take matters into my own hands. I nudge him along.

"So, tell me what happened. I'll just listen and remain neutral. There will be no judgment or advice. You and Lucy were serious, so for her to dump you—"

"I was the one who was the dumper." He drops a chunk of butter in the pan.

I pull on my earlobes in case I heard him wrong. "Excuse me?"

"I broke up with Lucy."

I know I said I'd listen; the experts recommend it. But it's impossible to remain neutral and not interject when a person drops a bombshell on you. Never did it cross my mind that *Austin* was the *dumper*. Once he commits, that's it. It's how he's been with everything from his job to his favorite movie. So though I know I need to remain quiet and just nod, let him continue leaning on me, he has made it impossible.

"What? Why? You were about to move in together! How do you go from moving in together to not being together at all?"

He pours egg in the sizzling skillet, prodding it with his spatula. "Like *you've* never dug in your heels to try to salvage something, even after you realize you'd misdirected your feelings?"

I kind of hate that he knows me so well and ponder my next words because obviously moving in together freaked Austin out to the point he broke up with Lucy. Part of me feels sad he ended their relationship just to avoid the commitment, and the other part is proud of myself that I didn't break up with Logan for the same reason. My metamorphosis is almost complete.

"Well, you could have fooled me," I say. "You seemed really happy."

I mean, they *did* fool me. I guess the old saying "appearances can deceive" applies to them. I've been so busy with my own love life, I clearly missed their demise. Charlotte had said things were strange at the bachelorette party, and I guess she was right. Is that why Lucy was all over him? Did she sense the end was near?

Once upon a time, pre-FriendsOfFriends, I would've been secretly thrilled that they broke up and twisted it into hope for me and him. But I've closed that door and even if I wanted to crack it back open, there's a big chance Austin would slam it in my face once he works through his commitment crisis. As a good friend, I need to put my personal feelings aside and help him see the error in his thinking.

Silence stretches between us until he finally looks up from the stove and stares at me for an awfully long time before speaking. "You seem happy, too."

Oh, no! Guilt shrouds me. I'm probably making him feel all sorts of jealous and sorrowful thinking about the happy relationship I'm in with Logan. I've been in that spot.

"Is anyone ever truly happy?"

"You're not happy?"

Maybe I should downplay it so he doesn't feel bad? Time to pull out my romance-novel acting skills again, because I possess no skills of my own to deal with his distress.

"Yeah, I'm happy. Some days..." I look down at my hands like Dakota in *Motorcycle Madness Book*

Ten: Mufflers of Desire. "Some days, I'm sad. Life is a mystery, Austin. Everyone must stand alone."

His brows raise as he slides a beautiful omelette onto a white plate and pours more eggs into the pan. "So you're not exclusive?"

Scoffing happens a lot in romance novels and I throw one in to be as vague and supportive as possible. "What's exclusive, anyway?"

"You'd turn down other dates." Oh. Well. I guess that one had a specific answer.

I think about his question while he finishes cooking. Logan and I may be having sex but neither of us have mentioned exclusivity. So it's hard to answer. Would I accept another date? If I say no, it's like I'm flaunting my relationship, kicking him while he's down. But I don't want to lie to Austin. And truly, in my heart, I know there is one circumstance that makes what I say next the truth.

"I suppose if the right one came along then...yes?"

He smiles and brings the plates over to the table. "All right. Awesome. Good to know."

I'm not sure exactly what happened there, except that I seem to have accidentally confirmed his commitment-phobic ways. But he seems to feel better, so there's no need to backtrack quite yet. I'll gently guide him around to my way of thinking, just like Dakota did when Nine-Iron got spooked at making her his old lady.

As we eat breakfast, I can't help but be proud of myself. Wow. I put my selfishness aside and eased his pain. I have evolved into an excellent friend.

THREE

TWO WEEKS IS WAY TOO long to be without *my* best friend. It's absolutely exhausting being caring all the time. I was growing desperate for a round of judgmental gossip. But at long last, Charlotte has returned from her honeymoon, having the absolute audacity to be tanned and gorgeous while I am still languishing in late-stage hibernation.

"How's Austin been?" she asks as we meander the aisles of Green Thumb, picking out items for the garden. "I still can't believe they broke up."

"Same. But he's surprisingly okay. I keep waiting for his change of heart, but so far it hasn't happened."

As we shop, I tell her about an awkward encounter when we ran into Lucy at the grocery store a few days ago. Austin decided he wanted to make lasagna for dinner and wanted me to come along with him to get the ingredients. It's unusual for me to accompany him, but he's probably subconsciously substituting me for what he doesn't have anymore. Probably the last time he does that, too, given how many interesting-looking things I threw in the cart for him to buy.

But then. In the fruit and vegetable section, there she was. Squeezing avocados, looking dazzling in a pink jogging suit and ponytail. There was not even a hint of regret in Austin's eyes when she spotted us and came over to say hi. And believe me, I watched closely from behind the banana display where I'd scurried off to so they could have privacy by the melons. Lucy acted a bit strange when Austin said we had to finish our shopping, but that was to be expected.

"Huh. Interesting," she says. "So what have you two been up to?"

"Without you around, I've devoted every ounce of my Be a Better Friend energy to nursing Austin through the breakup. He's really devoting himself to these garden plans." He's even drawn up a design and researched which spot in the backyard gets the most sunlight. "It's his breakup haircut I guess."

Charlotte laughs. "I guess we all handle things differently."

"Apparently." He hides his pain well. We've

watched movies, cooked together, worked on our art, and not a peep from him about feeling sad. He's even playing songs in major keys on his guitar. "I can't help but wonder how Lucy is doing. She seemed okay, but maybe she hides her pain well too."

"It's weird, huh? One thing about Lucy, she'll be okay. Guarantee it."

"Yeah." I inspect a garden gnome wearing a red hat. "We have to get this, right? As a reminder that if all else fails, we can always become ornamental garden-hermits."

Weird to think that conversation with Austin was almost a year ago. Even weirder that we are in such different places right now. I'm still not sure how to feel about the fact I started this journey to get over my crush, and he's now single.

"Absolutely," Charlotte says. "But grab him a few friends. He doesn't have to hermit for a paycheck."

"This is true."

We place the trio in the cart and wander around the warehouse-style building selecting a whole bunch of adorable ornamental things—an owl garden stake, a snail family, luxury bird feeder, cute signs for me to paint, and a must-have harvest basket for the bounty.

"This is going to be the best garden ever."

"Should we get more plants?" Charlotte asks, gazing at the lone purple flower in the cart.

"Possibly. And maybe some seeds?"

On our way back to the open-air floral section, she finally opens the can of worms. "So, at the risk of regretting it, I have to ask. What are *your* feelings about the breakup?"

I shrug. "My feelings are like a roller coaster without the screams."

"Hm," is all she says.

"That 'hm' means something." I stop near a display of monsteras. "Do you think I should break up with Logan?"

Her eyes widen to shocking proportions. "What? Why? Are you not happy? You seemed so happy."

"I am! I really am. It's just so hard not to wonder if my closure was premature."

"You did a closure?" She looks suspicious and I can't blame her. "*Hm.*"

"At your wedding. We held each other, and smelled each other's pheromones, and then bid them farewell. It was very cinematic; I'm surprised no one else noticed."

"Maybe Lucy did."

That bursts the feelings-dam I've been building out of denial and willpower.

"I mean, who says closure has to be final? Yes,

I'm really enjoying being with Logan, but you miss 100% of the shots you don't shoot, and what happens if I spend the rest of my life wondering why I didn't shoot when the shot was open, so to speak?"

"Excuse me," Charlotte says to a khaki-clad employee stacking sacks of potting soil, "I'm gonna need cleanup in Fertilizer after I murder my idiot friend."

Said employee pushes his oversized glasses up on his nose. "I don't want to be an accomplice to your crime. If you need help with anything else, let me know."

"She's kidding. Obviously. She'd need a better alibi than you," I assure him.

We move over to some hyacinths, and Charlotte continues to make sense. That jerk.

"Seriously, Chloe. You'd throw away Logan, the best boyfriend you've ever had, the drummer for Scarlet Letter, the only man on FriendsOfFriends who literally checks every single box of everything you want in a man...for the possibility of ruining your friendship with Austin with a rebound-bang?"

"Well, we haven't actually said the word *boyfriend* yet..."

And I'm still not bothered by that. Really, I don't even think about it. Unless I'm considering his plants, that is. We just kind of are what we are right now. We're both really busy and see each other when we can. There is no pressure. It's different from how I was always overanalyzing Finn, or chasing Dune, or getting low-key smothered by Ryan. Logan and I are just dating, like mature adults, and I'm not in a rush to make it more.

"Not the point," she says. "You have to know this relationship with Logan is going somewhere good. Finally."

"So...no to breaking up?" I mean. I wasn't exactly thinking of it as a real option, but without my bestie around to keep me grounded, how could I be certain?

Shooting shots and all that.

She places a pot with yellow flowers in the cart. "Take it from one who knows—you always hold on to a good thing when you find it."

She's right, and everything she says is spot-on. The indignant thump in my chest is just habit, nothing more. We closured for good. But we've been talking about Austin and also me for long enough. That's not how excellent friends behave.

"And how is married life?" I change the subject, selecting and then rejecting several plants of my own. "Do you feel different?"

"Well, speaking of seeds..."

"Charlotte," I laugh, "that is not how we refer to Mr. Charlotte's issuance." She picks up a bundle of baby's breath and a packet of cucumber seeds falls from my hand to the concrete floor. "Unless you mean…wait. You don't…?"

She looks at me from atop the flowers in her hand with unadulterated fear in her eyes. "Can we stop and grab a test after this?"

"Oh my God. Charlotte."

After *nothing*. There is no gnome more important than what's happening in her lady parts. We abandon our shopping cart and race off to the Target next door, only knocking the most sturdy-looking people aside in our haste to get to the correct aisle.

In the pharmacy, in front of the extensive variety of pregnancy tests, I take her hand. "Charlotte, what if? You'll be a great mom, I know it. But wow, a mom. The most important job in the world, and you might be hired for it."

"I would've liked an interview first," she says. picking up a box from the shelf and reading the back. "And maybe I'm just overreacting. My period is late, but that doesn't mean anything, right? It happens."

"How late?"

"Two months."

"Um…" So many ums.

"Ugh, I know. I thought it was stress from the wedding. But then it never came after the stress ended. So now I'm thinking it might not be the stress."

"Well, if you are, we're going to need a Pinterest board."

"Don't make me panic. I'm on the verge of panic, but I'm holding it back somehow. Barely. Let's just see what happens."

"Don't panic," I say. Target is not the place for a breakdown. "If anyone can do this, you can. Look at how well you take care of me. That should prepare you for anything."

"Can anyone prepare to never sleep again?" She proceeds to melt down in the pregnancy aisle. "I like sleeping. Love it so much. I could sleep for days sometimes, I just choose not to. And showering. I like being clean. I've seen those mom videos on social media. They're all complaining they never go to the bathroom in peace for like ten years. Ten years," her voice rises on that one. "I like going places alone when I want to go alone. I will never be alone again."

"Yes, you will. You'll still work and you'll get breaks."

"But it will all be scheduled. Freedom is gone. Do you understand that?

"You'll still have freedom. I'll help. Austin will help. Your parents will help. We're your village."

"My mom always said I'd be paid back for the

things I put her through when I have tiny Charlottes. Chloe, I was kind of a demon. What if I have Rosemary's baby?"

"Stop. I think parents tell you that to scare you. Granny Mae told me she had eyes in the back of her head and I believed it. I kept waiting to get mine before she finally told me it was a lie."

"I love her so much," Charlotte says. "Parents lie a lot to kids, don't they? I'm going to have to lie about Gentile Santa and the Passover Bunny. And the Tooth Fairy. Until one day their friends tell them I'm a liar. In first grade, my friend Dina believed in Santa until Morgan told her she was a baby and he wasn't real. I don't want to be a liar. And I refuse to do that creepy Elf on the Shelf. What psychopath thought of that?"

"Take a deep breath." She does. "Gentile Santa will not be an issue, and the Passover Bunny is just the excuse you made up to eat a pound of Peeps every spring. You're just freaking out. And that's okay. These are things you deal with when the time comes. Okay?" She nods. "And even if you did have Rosemary's baby, we'd love that little demon with all of our hearts. Forever and ever. Horns and all, Charlotte," I say. "We're gonna love it so hard we won't even think about the horns."

Her lip wobbles. "It's going to be okay?"

"Yes. You got this no matter what."

"I believe you," she says and takes another deep breath. "Let's do this."

After we purchase the test, the next stop is the bathroom to take it. Thankfully, it's empty. Charlotte rips open the box and heads into a stall.

I stand outside the door, trying to remain calm.

"It's gonna be a plus for yes, a minus for no. Easy to remember. Plus or minus. Plus or minus."

"Okay, got it. Plus or minus."

She accidentally drops the first in the toilet and I pass her the second, which she successfully pees on.

"Now we wait," she says.

A few painfully long minutes pass, and finally a result.

"Fuck," she says. "No way."

"What? Tell me. What does it say?"

"It's a division sign. I have a division sign," she yells. "What the fuck does that mean? All of the anticipation and I get a division sign?"

I scan the back of the box and there is no mention of division symbols, only plus or minus. What the hell? I do a quick internet search on my phone to see if anyone else had this problem, and of course, they didn't. Nothing. Nada. Zilch.

"You must be like one in a million. You sure it's a division sign? It says here that sometimes the line is really faint, so maybe you're misreading it. Like no one on the whole internet got a division sign. Isn't that unbelievable? You got the one wonky test in the billions produced. You sure it's not upside down or something?"

She sticks it out the door and yep, it's a division symbol. "Okay, well, hm. Maybe you're divided in your heart over how you feel. Or maybe it's like Schrodinger's fetus."

She steps out of the stall, frowning. "What the hell is that? Is it worse than Rosemary's baby?"

"You know, it's where it either is or is not a person, while a super early fetus, but whether it is a person can't be determined yet, because its future is unknown." She gives me a blank stare. "It's interesting to think about."

"I don't even know what that means, Chloe." A brunette enters the bathroom and side-eyes me as Charlotte shouts, "I'm going to need cleanup in the bathroom after I murder my idiot friend!"

I laugh. "...she's kidding..."

Hopefully.

FOUR

GARDENING IS A MISTAKE. This may be my worst idea yet. Logan is on a mini-tour, and will be back in nine weeks, so I have ample time to devote myself to keeping Austin busy. Ample time to rethink that decision, more like.

After Austin and I took a second, more productive, trip to the gardening store, purchasing seeds, plants, a variety of garden tools, fertilizer, and a few adorable decorative items, we made plans to spend the first warm day we have off together setting up the garden. That day is today. It's a balmy sixty degrees with a gentle breeze and a clear blue sky, perfect weather for planting things that apparently like to get snowed on before sprouting.

Plants are dumber than I am.

However, I wasn't prepared to see Austin sweating and lifting his shirt to wipe his brow. I've seen his abs more today than I have in five years. The little happy trail leading into his boxers has me feeling all kinds of things in my nether regions.

Not to mention the closeness as we dig rows, spread compost, and plant seeds side by side. Countless times our arms have brushed or our hands have touched. When I couldn't take the tingling sensations any longer, I tried moving away to my own area, but Austin foiled my attempt at distance. He thinks it's faster for us to work together. Maybe so, but it's certainly not easy, so when I am overwhelmed by his woodsy scent, and can no longer hold my breath, I escape his voodoo by checking my phone for a text from Charlotte. Today she has a doctor's appointment to confirm whether there is a baby or a mathematical operation growing inside her. So far, I've checked about a billion times because that's how much he affects me.

"Anything yet?" Austin asks, hoe in hand, looking unfairly masculine and handsome.

"Nope." I place my phone on the patio table and drag my ho feet back over to the back corner of the yard. "Must still be waiting to see the doctor."

After the fiasco in Target, Charlotte refused to

take another test, and instead made an appointment to have bloodwork at the OB-GYN's office. Waiting for information is excruciating for me, but I'm sure it's worse for her and Mr. Charlotte, so I'll have to suck it up.

"Ready to do the starters?" Austin asks. "How about vegetables?"

"Sounds good."

We gather the packets of seeds and tiny dirt discs that grow satisfyingly when you add water. Cucumbers, zucchini, and lettuce. Tomatoes and spinach, too. Maybe we are overly ambitious, but how could we turn down any seed's chance to grow and thrive and get eaten? After pushing eight zillion future foods into their little dirt homes, we move to doing the herbs. We plant basil, oregano, chives, and mint. All neatly labeled in Sharpie-on-masking-tape, which reminds me of Granny Mae so much I have to walk away again.

Getting her all-caps texts about THAT HUSSY NEXT DOOR is just not the same as helping her spy in person from her own garden.

"We're going to have a grocery store back here in the yard," I say.

"Yeah. Everything will taste so much better with fresh ingredients. I should've done this a long time ago," Austin says, reaching out to swipe the pad of his thumb across my cheek, burning my skin. "You had some dirt."

"Oh. I'm sure I'm filthy."

He swallows and reaches for his water bottle, taking a long swig. "I like that you're not afraid to get dirty."

Well, my *mind* certainly isn't afraid of getting dirty. It's been in the gutter for a week. My closure was exclusively emotional, and not at all physical, it turns out. Anything he says, my brain cells misfire and conjure up an illicit image. Like when we were watching TV last night, and he said watching me eat fettuccine was like food porn. I laughed, but hello! I had to pretend I was stuffed because I kept envisioning myself giving him a blowjob.

Logan being gone for nine whole weeks is turning me into a sex monster.

"Thanks for helping me," Austin says.

"You're welcome. I really need to go back for the gnome family now."

He chuckles. "That's probably still the creepiest thing you've ever told me."

"I feel like you're not appreciating garden life." I wave my hand around. "You wouldn't enjoy living amongst this beauty, letting your hair and nails grow long and tangled?"

"With you? Maybe."

He has no idea how the innocent things he says get twisted in my mind. He just means that hermit-buddies might be nice, but I am imagining garden sex now.

"What are you thinking about in that pretty head?" Austin asks.

I drop to my knees.

Luckily, I land by the tray of oregano starts. I pick them up like I totally meant to do that and not nearly fainting from his compliment. He thinks I'm pretty? In all the years I've known him, he's never said it in a general sense. Sure, he's told me I look beautiful, but that was when I asked how I looked in my Rose costume, forcing him to give me a positive answer. All men know that's the only correct answer. Except Adam, my two-week boyfriend in college, who told me I looked "all right."

"Babies," I say, hoping that scares him off so we don't have to talk anymore. Because between my overgrown fantasy life and his offhanded compliments, my closure is definitely reopening.

He crouches beside me. "What about them?"

I look over at him. This breakup has really got him inside out if he's not running from baby talk. Perhaps he's lonely? But if he's willing to listen, I'll take it because Charlotte's possible pregnancy also has *me* turned inside out.

"Well…Baby Charlotte is a life-changer." I sit cross-legged in the grass and let out my worries. "Am I ready? I feel like I need to be ready. My actions will influence a tiny human."

"What do you mean?"

I sigh. "This little person will be spending time with us and it's our responsibility to be good role models. I can't be the aunt without her shit together, ya know?"

He laughs. "You've got your shit together."

No, I really don't or I wouldn't be affected by how close he is right now or that he said my head is pretty. Normally, I don't need that type of validation, but when it comes from the mouth of someone I've fantasized my happiness ever-after with for so long… well, it's significant. Obviously, I know it means nothing to him. But it made butterflies swarm my belly when he said it and that's not good.

"Not really," I say. "I repeat my mistakes."

Affirming my statement, he drops down beside me, within inches, leaning back on his palms, stretching his long legs out, causing my heart to race. Our thighs brush, and I've never realized what a personal space invader Austin is until now. I do my best not to enjoy our closeness. I fail if anyone is keeping score.

"Don't say that. Look at what all you've accomplished." He peeks over at me. "I'm proud of you, Chloe. I don't think you realize how intriguing you are. I'm not sure if that's a good thing or a bad thing?"

Now it's my turn to ask, "What do you mean?"

"You're so fucking smart. Holding all that knowledge in your head. Do you have any idea how much I look forward to those nuggets of information?"

Gah. My heart is literally hurting, squeezing and aching, trying to beat its way out of my chest. And I know it's not heat exhaustion, because it's only March. Why must he say these things? I'm supposed to be propping him up, not the other way around.

"That's really sweet. Thank you. I think you're amazing too." Then I backtrack, "Well not that you said I was amazing."

His eyes sweep over my face. "You are," he murmurs. "Tell me something about gardening."

He's killing me today, and then I basically finish the job when I accidentally blurt out, "Did you know that May 2 is National Naked Gardening Day?"

His brow lifts. "Guess I know what I'll be doing on May 2."

Oh my. He's left me speechless, so I scoot closer to where we left off in the garden, needing space from this new Austin who says things like he'll be naked in the garden. He's like the serpent tempting me, and I don't know that I'm strong enough to resist.

We work in silence for a few minutes, watering the trays, and then he asks, "How many kids do you picture yourself with?"

"I don't have a perfect number in my head. Whatever I'm given, I guess." I glance up at him and immediately look away when I catch him staring at me. "I know you don't want kids, but—"

"I didn't *then*. They're not off the table now."

My gaze darts up to his. "Really? What made you change your mind?"

"I just think what's meant to be will happen. Can't run from fate." His fingers brush mine as he takes the watering can from me. "Things fall into place and the picture of what you want your life to look like becomes clearer. Plus, making them will be a whole lot of fun."

He winks, but I can hardly see it. I am overcome by a vision. An image of Austin having sex—with me—clouds my mind right before a brood of toothless babies toddle their way in to stop it. My face heats, and for fuck's sake, I'm blushing. These are not the types of conversations we had before he became single. His comment almost seemed flirtatious. Maybe he's got spring fever? It's not exactly spring yet, but the weather today feels like it, so maybe his body is confused.

Or maybe not having Lucy around has made him a sex monster, too. That would be very, very bad.

"Did I just make you blush?" he says, horrifying me.

"Maybe."

"Sorry." Finally, he gives me a reprieve and moves away. "I guess we're finished here. Want to go inside for lunch?"

Not if it's sandwiches. There's no way I can take him saying things about shoving the best meat in me right now. My body is buzzing like a live wire from this whole experience. And that was not a supportive-friend reaction. I said goodbye yet all it takes is a few questionable comments from him and I'm ready to return to clinger status. Not good. Not good.

Curse my sinful nature, and my repeated mistakes!

"Okay." I stand and try not to stare at the sexy smudge of dirt on his cheek, just above the scruff covering his jaw.

That's another thing. Is he growing back his beard? If so, there's no way I can live here. But I have to, dammit. I have to control myself. *Get it together, Ho-e.*

I'm not the same starry-eyed girl from a year ago. I've grown in ways I don't even realize. I am an excellent goddamned friend. I keep telling myself that as he does indeed prepare us sandwiches, caressing my bread like a lover.

"So why is Logan gone so long?" he asks, drizzling olive oil over the sliced tomatoes.

"They're playing at a new bar franchise that launched across the country. They'll be traveling from state to state performing at the openings."

"Cool," he says. "Glad I got you all to myself."

"That you do."

He talks about the restaurant as we eat lunch, and then I clean the kitchen as best I can with him everywhere I turn. It's important for me to ease his load during this time and take on my share of the cleaning, but like in the garden, I'm hyper-aware of his closeness. Maybe he doesn't know how to be alone now and just needs to be in my presence as some sort of security blanket? Whatever his reason, it's messing with my head.

My phone chimes and I yank it out of my pocket.

I stare at the screen. And then a tear trickles down my cheek.

"Charlotte is for real pregnant," I whisper.

"Wow," he says. "Really?"

"The doctor confirmed it, so it must be true."

"Fuck. A baby. I can't believe it."

"Yeah. You can't curse anymore. You'll have to spell it out."

Wow. She's going to be a mom. And I'm going to be an aunt. Holy Have to Be Responsible. I'm really an adult now.

FIVE

ADULTING IS HARD. Once you're in it, there's no turning back to simpler times when you lounged and handed out rocks to strangers on a dating site. Now that I'm officially a responsible human, in a jarring twist of events, time is hurtling by at warp speeds. This not-enough-hours-in-the-day must be a cruel joke from the universe to speed up the aging process. Swear I found a new line beside my eye when I smiled for a selfie to send Logan.

A couple of weeks have passed since my passage into the grownup phase of life, and I've been so busy, I barely have time to miss him. It's a full-time job juggling all the balls I have in the air. And not the man-balls I've become an expert at handling. On top of creating a Baby Charlotte-to-be Pinterest board and updating it daily, tending to Austin's fragile state along with the garden, and working at It's Clay Time, my Mae'd With Love business is booming.

The web sales are growing at a rapid pace and Mildred just gave me a phone order for another hundred mugs to restock the boutique for an upcoming Spring window display at Something Borrowed.

It's all a little more to handle than I anticipated, but isn't everything? My mom saying I'd understand someday why she was too busy to drop everything on a whim and take me to the mall for the Bob Ross lunchbox I wanted suddenly makes sense. I really need to hire someone else, because the work is getting overwhelming, but I'm still *this* far away from having enough money to justify it even though I know I'd be able to produce more product if I brought in someone to help me.

It's F-U-C-K-I-N-G exhausting.

After I log Mildred's new order in my spreadsheet, it's time to make a call I've been putting off because I've been so overwhelmed already.

The husky voice I haven't heard since last summer answers on the second ring. "Chloe?"

"Hello, Dune."

"Are you finally taking me up on the booty call?"

I laugh, as does he, in a good-natured way. "Sorry,

no." But I plan on taking him up on his friend's discount.

"That's too bad," he says with a smile in his voice. "How have you been?"

"Good," I say, amazed at my ability to have a civil conversation with an ex-boyfriend. I'd probably still be just all right to Adam, though. "How's life treating you? Still living on the edge?"

"Can't complain. I'm on a ride with the brothers out in California. Finally, I swam with sharks."

"Wow, really? How was it?"

His commitment to endangering his life is admirable.

"It was amazing. You would've loved it."

Ha. His statement is proof he never knew me. "Doubtful, but I'm glad you got to check it off your list. Did you know California has one of the highest concentrations of sharks in the world?" Which is why I'm content swimming in a pool if I ever go there.

He chuckles. "I probably should have known that, but I swam first and asked questions later."

Our conversation drifts to catching up on life that's transpired since our breakup. He tells me that a pet psychic suggested Coco start going on hikes with him. He puts her in a little backpack and she frightens off bears with her face. He didn't say the part about the bears, but it's probably true. He tells me Angel and Jackal got engaged and I tell him about Charlotte's wedding and Mae'd With Love's success. It's all very adult.

"That's awesome," he says. "Hope you're using a spreadsheet to keep track of your finances."

"I am. Speaking of finances...are you still available to do my taxes?"

"Absolutely," he says. "And don't forget the discount for bringing friends."

"Thank you." I smile, because truly, it feels like Dune is a friend too. And I'm glad. Like Ryan, just because we didn't work out in a romantic sense doesn't mean we don't work as friends. Granny Mae always says to surround yourself with people you wouldn't mind getting stuck on a desert island with and I agree.

I've never remained friends with my exes, and I'm certain this is another symptom of my new level of adulthood. I'm so mature.

By the time we're off the phone, and I've mentally patted myself on the back a few more times, I've scheduled an appointment in a couple of weeks for myself, Charlotte, and Austin.

I've hardly set the phone down when it buzzes with a text from Ryan.

Is it Ex-Boyfriend Day? Nothing on the calendar.

It might be a moon sign thing, though. The text says to check my email, which I do. Gasp.

He's forwarded an opportunity to apply for a curator position at a gallery in Santa Fe, New Mexico that I would never have the guts to apply for if not specifically recommended to it.

"These are the responsibilities I'm looking to fill in this curator position," a man named Dominic says in the email.

I scan the list he's provided to see what I can check off within my capabilities.

Managing new collections by recording and cataloging artwork. (Check.)

Researching objects to document identification and authentication. (Check. Check.)

Planning and executing exhibitions, including the presentation of artwork, as well as writing acquisition and exhibition proposals. (Check. Check. Check.)

"Training of staff on the exhibition's presentation and information is involved," he writes, "so they'll need to be a people person. I know you're an artist with connections, so if you know anyone qualified, send them my way."

It's a dream job. And as the email chain reads, Ryan has already recommended me to the owner, whom he knows. How did I get so lucky in the ex-boyfriend department? Even if I don't pick good boyfriends, I sure pick good ones to break up with.

"I think this position suits you and your knowledge. Dominic is a great guy," Ryan says in the forward. "We did ayahuasca together at an art retreat. I'd trust him with my life. Don't ever bring up monkeys around him, though."

"Thank you for recommending me, Ryan," I reply. "I'll be sure to never mention that Alexander I, the king of Greece, died from sepsis after one of his pet monkeys bit him."

I slam my laptop shut. This is...wow. Just wow. I don't have time to process this opportunity because I've got to start throwing my next round of plates for Mae'd, but...boy, the thought of leaving this stress for the job of my dreams is a fantasy I can get behind.

For now, I can only get behind the pottery wheel to fill more orders. I ready the clay and when the phone rings again, I half worry it'll be Finn, but luckily, it's Logan calling from Albuquerque.

Is it a *sign*? The universe needs a decoder ring.

"Hey, you," he says. "What's up?"

"Just doing some work." I tuck the phone between my shoulder and cheek so I can multitask and throw clay while talking, because that's how behind I am. "What's up with you?"

"Well," his voice lowers to a seductive hush, "if you really want to know...my dick."

"Oh my." A current zips to my core upon hearing his dirty words. I'm not a sexpert on the phone and it certainly shows in my next question. "Do you need to do something about...that?" So far, since he's been away, our phone conversations have been brief, and certainly not naughty, so this is unexpected.

"Yeah," he says, breathing a bit heavier. "I'm so horny. Are you alone?"

Austin isn't home, but I feel like he is, so I whisper, "Yes. Tell me more."

I nearly spin the clay off the wheel when he says,

"I've had this ache in my cock for weeks. Even my balls ache. And I'm lying here in the hotel room," he moans, "stroking myself. It would turn me on so much more if you were touching yourself too."

"That's so hot," I murmur. "Continue."

There's no reason I can't finish this plate while he pleasures himself. It's not like he'll know I'm fondling clay instead of myself.

"I'm thinking about your pussy, how tight and trimmed it is, and how I'd love to be in it right now."

"Yeah?" Gah. The erotic sounds he's making have me squirming in my seat, but I just need a couple more minutes to finish this plate. The wheel whirls and my hands glide along the wet clay as I stall for time. "What else are you thinking about?"

My tactic works. Phone sex is pretty easy. You just ask a lot of questions.

"I'm thinking about you licking this pre-cum off the head of my dick. I'm rubbing it with my thumb, imagining it's your tongue."

He groans so loud, an earthquake of desire rumbles through my body. Screw the plate. I wash my hands and power walk to my bedroom. Though I wasn't prepared for phone sex, and this isn't my niche, my inner sex monster can wait no more.

"Keep talking," I say. "It's so sexy you're touching yourself." A clear vision of him jerking off forms in my mind.

"What are you wearing?"

"Black joggers and a green hedgehog T-shirt."

"Mm," he says.

I lock my bedroom door and cross to the bed, climbing on top of the comforter, ready to play. "Really? Should I have made something up that's sexier? Like, is that part of the fantasy and I should tell you I'm wearing a French maid outfit, watering your plants?"

"Nope. The only thing that would be sexier is if you were naked. What color are your panties?"

"Pink," I answer.

"Fuck. I love pink panties." He pants a little into the phone, and I lie back, closing my eyes, letting his sounds turn me on and ease my stress. "Is it a thong, settled between your ass cheeks?"

I stick with the truth, even if he seems excited at the prospect of ass floss. "No, ugh. They're bikini panties with a little bow in the center."

"Mm. I love bows on panties. What does your bra look like?"

I really need to buy some more of the good ones. "Pink with a little bow in the center," I fib, because the ol' white sports bra is just not sexy.

"Ah, I love it. Wish I could see it." Please don't let him ask for a picture. He doesn't, thank God. "Touch yourself for me. Tell me if you're wet."

I plant my feet on the bed and slide a hand down my stomach into my panties. "Yeah, I'm wet. So wet." Is that enough? I throw another one in for good measure. "So very wet."

"Damn. My cock is throbbing."

I moan, imagining his thighs quivering as he fists himself.

"Squeeze your nipples and think about me taking them in my mouth. Mm. Sucking until you beg me to fuck you. Biting and licking until you come." He groans and I do what he asks, squeezing the hardened peaks, losing my inhibitions in the shamelessness of masturbating with him.

Phone sex is fun and naughty, the perfect way to distract me...and also lonely.

As much as I'm enjoying this, my touch isn't the same. There's no tongue or stubble to heighten the sensation. There are no deep kisses to make my heart pound out of my chest. And after all the time I've spent with Austin lately, I can't help but picture him instead of Logan.

The vision of Austin tormenting me won't go away as I edge myself closer to orgasm, moving my fingers faster as Logan says filthy things into my ear as he jerks off.

"I'm going to come, Chloe," he says, grunting and filling the phone with sensual sounds.

I've reached new lows when I imagine that Austin is the one groaning in my ear as I come too.

When our pants subside, he says, "That was phenomenal. Let's do this again."

"Yeah, let's." Hopefully, that didn't sound as unenthusiastic to him as it did to me.

Why do I feel like an entire year's progress just collapsed into a lump of clay? At least the only rocks in my life now are in the garden.

SIX

LOGAN HAS BEEN GONE for more than a month and my thoughts are growing ominous. Are we even still dating? We talk to each other at least every other day for a few minutes, and have phone sex probably once a week, but I'm too nervous to find out he's banging roadies so I don't bring anything like that up when he calls me.

And I'm certainly not bringing up that more times than not, someone else occupies the space in my head when I orgasm during our pseudo-sex sessions.

Through the window over the kitchen sink, I watch Austin unroll the hose so he can water the garden. Lean muscles ripple beneath his blue T-shirt as he jerks at a tangle to free it, giving me fodder for more phone sex fantasies. *Stop it, Chloe*, I whisper to myself, and dump my coffee into the sink when Austin catches me staring and smiles.

I'd like to say I don't give a toothy grin back, but I can't. This is *not* how adults act. Maybe I'm destined to forever be a child in a woman's body. I hope someone lets my crow's foot know. With a sigh, I move over to my laptop and check my email.

Exclamation points pop in my head when I see the gallery owner scheduled an interview.

"Just a formality," he assures in his brief email. "I'd trust Ryan with my life. Great guy. If you ever find yourself in some monkey business…"

My fingers shake as I type my reply, thanking him profusely for the opportunity and hoping I win bonus points by assuring him I steer clear of primate nonsense.

"Our babies are starting to grow," Austin says, bounding in the back door, bringing the scent of sunshine and forbidden fantasies with him.

"It's adorable how excited you are about homegrown cucumbers and tomatoes," I say.

He grins. "Can't wait for the first harvest."

"What are you going to make?" I hit send on my email and close my laptop.

He lounges back against the counter, resting his palms on the granite. Our little sprouts are indeed growing, on every windowsill, and some in the patch outside too. "The best salad you've ever had."

"Hm. Really? I don't know if a salad is as satisfying as say…pasta?"

"Chloe," he makes a tsk sound, "have I taught you nothing? Let me show you how fantastic salad can be." He strolls to the fridge and opens it.

"Well, not to salad-shame, but they're all kind of the same."

"I disagree." He turns around with his hands full of items and I watch as he arranges them on the counter before grabbing two white plates from the cabinet. "Come here."

Oh dear. The way he says it, bossy, with a glance at me beneath his lashes, has me complying with his directions.

"Yes, sir," I say.

His dark eyes flare, and his sultry gaze drops to my mouth for a beat before he continues with his show-and-tell, splitting open the head of greenleaf lettuce with his hands. "I'll admit a salad can be boring if it's not done right. I'll even go so far as to say you've probably had a good salad. Probably even thought it was great. And most likely it was because that's all you knew at the time. You had nothing to compare it to." He glances down at me. "But it wasn't the best. And you know why?"

I shake my head, unsure if we're really talking about salad. "No. Why?"

"Because it wasn't my salad."

Seconds tick away as we stare at each other. "I'd like to have your salad."

He mesmerizes me with a rake of his teeth across his bottom lip before he selects a knife from the block. "We don't just eat with our taste buds, Chloe. Our minds have a big say in whether we enjoy something."

Don't I know it. "I can see that."

He fondles a ripe tomato. "Vegetables can be sexy. You need to handle them right."

I'll agree with that statement. Especially when it's held in his hand. "You have to grip the tender flesh, firm but gentle enough not to bruise."

I'll never make it out of this salad lesson alive. He makes a cut. "See the juices?"

"Yeah, the juices are flowing," I murmur.

He scoops up a generous handful of lettuce and drops it on the plate. "I want to fill you up, so I'm going to spread it wide."

"Yes, wide is good. I need a lot of salad to satisfy me." His fingers pause their foreplay in the greens. "I mean...yeah, looks good."

While I try to calm my erratic heartbeat, he swiftly slices the tomato and a few kalamata olives, crumbles some feta. When he gets to the cucumber, it's impossible to even breathe. "Here." He holds it out. "Feel this."

"Um, okay." I take the cucumber from him and hold it in my palm.

"How would you describe it?"

"It's hard and long..." I slide my hand down the green length. "Thick."

He snatches it from me and blows out a breath. "It's got nothing on mine."

I need Tattoo Jesus. It's like sex the way he carries on describing the amazing salad he's going to make when the garden is ready. Because he was definitely talking about our home-grown cucumber and not the one in his pants. Right? He uses words like *sweet*, *spicy*, *tantalizing*, and a myriad of others that have me clenching my thighs in anticipation of what he's going to say next. And when I nearly have a mini-orgasm, he finishes me off with a douse of homemade vinaigrette, splashed over everything.

"And that's how you make a salad."

I'll say. Hope it was as good for him as it was for me.

I polish it off in record time, and as I'm debating whether or not to lick the plate, he asks if I want to help find homes for our gnomes. And even though I do not have time to frolic in the Garden of Sin with the gigantic amount of mugs I have to glaze this weekend, I cannot say no to gnomes.

I'm pulling on my gardening boots (I have gardening boots now, *so* legit) when the doorbell rings. Without peeping to see who is on the other side, I swing the door open to find Lucy with a hand resting on her shapely hip.

"Hi," I say, and immediately realize that I have been lying to myself.

The knotted-stomach feeling I get when I see Lucy's hair shining in the midday sun is upsetting. I've told myself I've moved on from Austin so often I had started to believe it. I just miss Logan, I told myself. I'm just being a good friend, I said. But the jealousy turning me pea green says otherwise.

"Hey, Chloe. Is Austin here?"

Just as I'm getting ready to invite her inside, Austin says from behind me, "Oh, hi. You don't have to come in. I put the stuff you asked for in a box already."

He hands her a small brown box. Lucy looks just as surprised as I feel.

"Just as well, I have a date to get ready for," she says.

I grip the doorknob, bracing for Austin's jealousy. "Cool," he says, with no emotion. "You already look perfect."

She blinks at his dismissal as Austin moves past her onto the porch and sits in the swing to tug on his gardening boots.

Lucy smiles, but it doesn't reach her eyes. "Okay, talk later. Bye, Chloe."

"Bye," I say as she leaves without a glance backward.

When her car is out of the driveway, Austin grabs the bucket we keep the hoes in. "Ready?"

"Um, yeah."

I search his face for any sign he's masquerading and putting on a show to hide regrets behind his handsome face, but there's nothing to suggest he's hiding any second thoughts about breaking up with Lucy.

"Let's do it."

I ignore my dirty mind, and we head to the backyard, to put our ornamental hermits into their private oasis. While we test out different groupings around the beds, I tell him about the interview I'm going to have for the curator job.

"Seriously? That's amazing."

"I'm just nervous." I pull a little weed from near the tomato stakes. "It's been ages since I've interviewed. And never for something this important. You know this was always my dream."

"You got this. I'll help you practice."

"Okay, but really stick it to me."

"I'd love to." He's arranged the gnome triad near the lattice his highly anticipated cucumbers will climb. Backs together, so they cannot be surprised by any hungry rabbits. They'll see everything coming. Smart. He stands from his stooped position and pulls me up. "Thank you for coming in today."

"My pleasure."

"So, tell me what your five-year plan is."

"Oh, well, first let me just say I love your office."

He grins. "Thanks, my lovely assistant helped me decorate."

"I'm sure she's amazing."

"Let me tell you a secret about her." He leans closer, and my heart races. "She's the most amazing person I've ever met."

"I'm sure you're an amazing boss."

He steps closer, too close for comfort. But I don't move away. "I'll have to ask her if she thinks I'm amazing. What do you think she'd say?"

He tucks a strand of hair behind my ear and trails a finger around the shell. "She'd probably say if this is how you interview, you might find yourself in the human resources office."

We both laugh and then it dies in the warm breeze. And then suddenly we're kissing.

I didn't see that coming.

With one hand cradling my face, the other on my ass pulling me in closer, he sprinkles soft kisses on my mouth and then tugs my bottom lip.

"I've been dying to kiss you again," he rasps.

"Austin," I whisper, as the hand on my back slides up my back, into my hair.

The gentle kisses slowly grow more urgent, and on a groan, he slides his tongue into my mouth. I'm melting, clinging to him, returning his kiss with desperation. It feels like I'm in the middle of a rainstorm, drowning.

His body melds to mine, and he holds on to me like I'll disappear if he lets go. It's a serious kiss, a needy kiss, a kiss that makes every fine hair on my body stand on end, and goes on for a while, but not long enough, before I remember I might actually be cheating.

And also, why is Austin making out with me? And now that I think about the way he's been acting around me lately, like that dinner he made for just the two of us a couple of nights ago, with wine and candles...

"Are you *dating* me?" I pull away and ask.

He drops his forehead to mine, breathing heavy. "I'm trying to."

"Do you...like-like me?"

"That's kind of what kissing means." He leans in to kiss me again.

I back up. "We kissed before and it didn't mean that."

"It did. But we weren't ready."

I need a thesaurus because all I can think is wow. Oh, wow. Wow.

"...Did you break up with Lucy because of...?" I can't even be presumptuous enough to finish the sentence.

He nods. "Lucy and I hadn't been working for a long time. It became more obvious that it wasn't going to get better when I realized I was having feelings for someone else."

"By someone else you mean...me?" I need this to be real clear.

He makes it crystal clear. "Yes, Chloe. I mean you. I thought maybe...am I wrong? Am I too late?"

I almost blurt out that no, he wasn't wrong and of course he isn't too late, but I've matured in this last year. I know better than to be impulsive. I can't think straight right now, and I really, really need to consider all of this.

"I need to think," I say, instantly hating the disappointment in his eyes. "I should go wash up."

My feet only take two steps before I turn back to

him. "Maybe we should have a real date?" Okay, I'm still sort of impulsive.

"Okay. Will you go on a real date with me?" What am I *doing*?

"Actually, I still need to think," I say. "I haven't done the thinking yet."

God, I'm a mess.

He nods. "I respect that. Take all the time you need. If you want to talk about things, I'm here."

I do want to talk, but it's best not to do it when I'm still under the effects of an unforgettable kiss. Plus, I have to try to get some work done before I get showered and changed and drive down to Colorado Springs. Because guess what's happening tonight?

I'm going to see Logan play a show.

SEVEN

WALT WHITMAN SAID IT BEST...

Do I contradict myself?
Very well then I contradict myself,
(I am large, I contain multitudes.)

It's a great quote and sounds exactly like me. All I've wanted is Austin, and now that he wants me, I suddenly don't know what I want anymore. You'd think I'd leap at the chance to date him. But it's complicated, and that kiss—that kiss!—complicated it more.

After I showered and dressed, I exited my room to find him gone so I spent some time searching the internet for advice. The experts all said what I already know.

It's possible to care about two people at once, and apparently my brain is pumping out dopamine for both guys. I'm just not sure what to do. Things are still new with Logan, but the non-pressure situationship we're in right now feels good. Like taking things slow and really getting to know each other is how to build a solid foundation for something that will last. Dammit, FriendsOfFriends, those rocks were apt after all.

But Austin. He makes me feel safe, like I'm already on solid ground. Our foundation is friendship. It's like a favorite sweater that has weathered storms with you and fits like none of the new ones. It's a deep connection for me with Austin, but that doesn't mean it is for him. He just left a long-term relationship, and I know exactly how rebounds work. If I jump into something with him and it falls apart after a season, so will our little friend group.

So, the truth is, I'm terrified. Austin holds the power to hurt me in a way I've yet to experience. Dune's poem flits through my mind. If only I knew which path to take. Do I choose to slam the brakes and end the possibility of letting him in or do I go for it? Both guys have their positives and I don't know which man to choose.

And taking the dream job in Santa Fe might mean choosing neither.

I don't know the answer; it's nerve-wracking. So I do the only thing I can think of in my time of confusion. I FaceTime Granny Mae in the parking lot of Logan's venue so she can advise me.

"Do you need help, Chloe? Blink your eyes if you need me to call 911."

"I haven't been kidnapped!"

"Then why are you FaceTiming looking so upset in a shifty-looking car?"

I spend the next five minutes assuring her nothing nefarious has happened to me. "See..." I get out of my shifty car and show her my surroundings, nicer cars and people walking toward the bright lights of Neon Nights. "Everything is fine. I just need your wisdom."

She nods. "What's wrong, honey?"

I lean against the car. "How do you know someone is the one?"

Her phone nearly touches her nose. "Are you in love, Chloe?"

"Well...there're two guys—"

"Two?"

I tell her about Logan and how we met.

"Let me guess...the other is Austin?"

My brows raise because I've never confessed my crush to her. "How did you know?"

"Because you're my *blood* and when you talk

about him, you get a look in your eye that's unmistakable. I know he's got a girlfriend, but I've been rooting for you two for years."

She listens, without judgment, as I explain his breakup with Lucy and what transpired when I fell from grace in the garden. Minus the explicit details, because I'm not that kind of a monster.

"Ah," she says, as if I should know what that means.

"Tell me what to do. Am I a rebound? Do I end the good thing I've got going and risk ruining my friendship with Austin if things don't work out? Is it against the rules to date two people? I know you're not dating, but—"

"Chloe, I'm going to tell you something. I signed up on that dating site of yours."

Oh.

My.

Gawd.

"Granny Mae," I squeal. "You're dating? On the internet? But it's full of weirdos!"

"Don't be so old-fashioned. Everyone dates on the internet now. Found out at Bingo that Ruth signed up too. Of course she did. Always wanting what's mine. My point is...we hold all kinds of love in our hearts but love is different from chemistry and it's important not to confuse them."

"What do you mean?"

"Obviously it's good to have chemistry. But chemistry is just that. A reaction in your body." I'm not sure I'm ready to hear Granny Mae's birds-and-bees talk but I remain silent as she goes on.

"It can make smart people do dumb things. I've been out with a few men and we've had chemistry." Or Granny Mae's girl-talk. "It's exciting, but confuses your brain into thinking you're in love. You feel consumed by it, but that's just the chemical reaction. Love is deeper. It develops over time. Like me and your grandfather. It endures, even after they're gone."

Aw. I want to reach through the phone and hug her. "I hope you find another love."

"Maybe I will. I accepted a rock from a guy named Barnabus. I play Bingo with his sister. She makes a mean potato casserole."

"Yeah?" I smile. Coming from Granny Mae, who firmly and rightly believes her own recipes are always best, that's a good sign. "Don't do anything I wouldn't do."

Immediately I regret saying that, because I do everything.

Well, almost everything.

Some things should be saved for true love, which is how I know that Jesicha is going to agree to betray her MC for Tombstone in the Motorcycle Mayhem book I'm currently reading.

"We're going to go to dinner. If I don't like him, I'm sure Ruth will take him. She always wants my rejects."

I laugh. "Maybe you two can double date and end the war."

"Never," she says.

We talk a while longer, and then I tell her I have to get going.

"You just take your time and you'll know what's right," she says. "Open your heart, let yourself be vulnerable. Love is a choice, in a sense. And you'll make the right one."

"Well, I don't know about that."

"Date them both. Why do you have to choose just one to date? I'm not going to. If society doesn't like it, well, they need to get the stick out of their butts. They don't pay your bills to have a say, now do they?"

I laugh, but it's true. As always, her advice changes my perspective.

Instead of seeing it as something bad within *me*, I should realize that something is missing with Logan and I'm not fully invested, or I wouldn't be kissing Austin in the garden.

Rather than end things with either, I need to

empower myself to make the best choice for me. And if that means having a *Bachelorette* moment to date them both, maybe I should just do it.

"Thank you, Granny Mae. I love you."

"Love you too. Oh, and I'm going to place an order on your website tomorrow. It's come to my attention that the Ladies Club needs new serving dishes, and it'll really raisin Ruth's cookie to see my recipes on every one. Toodles!" She ends the call, blissfully unaware that although she'd lightened the load on my heart, she'd also just increased the load that really might break my back soon.

Rather than dwell on work, I just check my mascara in the side mirror one last time and head inside to see Logan. I'm feeling a tiny bit nervous. What if, after all this time apart, our chemistry is gone? What if he really only *did* want a steady lay to water his plants? What if he has one in every port—er, gig stop?

Those fears are hardly even full-grown before Logan squashes them. He's waiting for me by the bouncer, looking absolutely delicious and clearly appreciating the low-cut top I'm wearing.

"Was I right or what?" he asks the bouncer, never taking his eyes off me as he walks forward to grab my hands and look me up and down.

"You were right," the hulking dude says, never

actually looking at me at all. "Prettiest girl I ever saw."

He moves on to flirting with the guy that walked in just behind me, and Logan moves *us* on, leading me through the venue and out the stage door.

"When the van is rocking, no one will come knocking," he says, pulling me into the Scarlet Letter minivan to bang pre-show.

"You sure?" I say, glancing over my shoulder at the back door of the venue.

"Positive."

Before I can object or think about my confusion regarding Austin, his lips are attached to mine. I can't help comparing kisses as his tongue meets mine. Logan's is wonderful, don't get me wrong, but it doesn't set my soul on fire and threaten to spread like a wildfire until I'm nothing but charred ashes.

But maybe if I give him a chance, it will?

Or am I mistaking chemistry for love with Austin's all-consuming passion?

"Fuck, there's not a lot of room in here," he says, pulling me into his lap, and sliding his hand up my skirt with nimble fingers. I have no Austin memory to compare this to, and that's fine by me. Less confusing. And also, he is really good at this. I have very much missed the touch of a hand that isn't mine.

"We have to hurry because the show starts soon

and I have to warm up with the band." He's sure warming me up. But I should say something, I really should.

"So, I was thinking—" He sucks my earlobe into his mouth, and I moan, completely unable to finish my thought about staying non-exclusive.

"No thinking," he says, moving from my earlobe to much further south. "Just feel."

Oh, and I do. For the very brief moment that it lasts. This is not the ideal place for sex. The van is a little crowded with band stuff...and messy. I kneel on a discarded water bottle, or something equally crunchy, as I try to gracefully move to the top in our tight space so he can unzip and push down his jeans to roll a condom onto his hard length.

We moan in unison as he eases into me.

Should I feel guilty? This definitely feels good. If I wasn't into him anymore, it wouldn't feel good, right? Anger drives my hips down in a frenzy as I ride him in the back of the van, holding the back of the seat, releasing my frustrations with every thrust from Logan.

"You're so sexy right now," he says, watching our bodies connect.

Confusion is as terrible as guilt. Why now, when I've finally met a decent guy, does Austin decide he wants to date me? I was half hoping the sex would be bad and that would be an indicator that I should go out with Austin and dump Logan, but Logan and I still have all the chemistry we ever had. Which leaves me in limbo.

What if I give up this good thing and Austin loses interest?

When Logan presses the pad of his thumb to my clit, rubbing the bundle of nerves, I force myself to focus on him, the way he pants, the lusty haze in his eyes when he stares back at me, the sexy way he bites his lip, because I don't want to close my eyes and chance Austin slipping into my mind.

He rams faster into me, with no mercy, until my orgasm sneaks up and my hand Rose-slaps against the fog-covered window as I shatter into blissful pieces.

"Oh God," he says, pumping faster until a shudder wracks his body and he releases a moan loud enough to alert the whole bar to our shenanigans.

A knock raps on the passenger window on the opposite side of the van. "Dude, are you fucking?" Will's voice says.

"Oh God," I echo, climbing out of Logan's lap, bumping my head on the ceiling, pulling my skirt down. "Someone did come knocking."

"Nobody's home," Logan calls out.

"Open the door. I won't look," he says.

"Such a pervert," Logan shoots back.

Within a few minutes, we're presentable, and I climb out.

"Oh, hi. We were just talking. Catching up a bit."

Will smirks. "Mm-hmm." He waves a finger at my shirt. "You might want to fix that."

I look down at my left boob, thankfully still in its bra, but completely outside of the shirt. Lovely.

"What do you want?" Logan asks, joining me outside the van.

"Just need my throat coat tea." Will leans in and produces a crumpled box. "You smashed it, asshole."

Their friendly bicker continues as we walk toward the building, and after a few minutes, Logan leaves me with a kiss on the forehead to go warm up with the band.

When the show starts, I join Belinda at a spot in the corner to enjoy the music and people-watch. The crowd sings along, and a bevy of girls gyrate to the beat. The guys give an amazing performance and after, smile while they're mauled by press and fans. Really, is this point in Logan's life the time for him to be in a relationship?

Although Will and Belinda still grin at each other like they're as smitten as the day they met.

"Are we exclusive?" I ask Logan backstage after they've finished.

He must be tempted by the attention he receives, right? As I know, dating someone doesn't make you not feel attraction to another person, unplanned or not.

"Yeah," he says, "were you worried I was banging other girls on tour?"

Um. "You can!"

"You want me to?" His brow furrows. "This isn't how I thought things were going with us..."

I sigh. "That's not...you know what, I want a do-over of this conversation after I've rehearsed."

"Rehearsed?" He crosses his arms. "What are you saying?"

I lower my voice, because we aren't exactly alone for this incredibly awkward moment. "Nothing," I say. "I'm not saying anything. Let's talk tomorrow. I need to get on the road."

"You're sure you can't stay the night with me?"

"I'm afraid I'll hit that storm that's coming in, and I have a birthday party at It's Clay Time in the morning."

I've been really good about being a responsible employee at these work events since the last time. And even if I called in, I have my tax interview with Dune right afterwards, so there's really no way.

We still kiss goodbye, but it's weird now. It's going to be a long drive home in more ways than one.

EIGHT

SOMETIMES I FEEL like my life isn't real and I'm living in a cartoon. At any moment, an anvil is going to drop from the blue sky, landing on me, squashing me into the grass beneath my sneakers.

"Are you sure this is a good time?" I ask Dune as he leads us past the row of shiny motorcycles parked at Pres's house onto the wide front porch I love so much.

"Nothing is certain except death and taxes," he answers. "That's a motto I try to live by."

I'm fairly certain I might die before Dune finishes squaring up my IRS obligations. We arrived to find out it's picnic day in biker land and although it was nice catching up with Dune's people and partaking in a few deviled eggs for old time's sake, Coco was not happy to see me again.

My presence has sent her into a feline frenzy of passive-aggressive behavior. She stalks our quartet through the spacious living room with a scowl on her misshapen face, no doubt plotting how to claw out my eyes.

As we pass a massive painting of the skull MC logo hanging above the fireplace, Austin glances over at me with a look that says he doesn't want to be here. Ever since we arrived, he's been on edge, stuck to my side as if he needs to be ready to protect me at any moment.

"We can reschedule if you need to get back to your picnic," he says to Dune's leather-vested back. "They really wanted you for that knife-throwing contest."

"No, it's cool," Dune says, leading us down a tiled hallway into a large office with a gigantic mahogany desk. "Still haven't won my house back so we can do business here in Pres's office." He arranges padded chairs in front of the desk.

"That's unfortunate about your house," I say, alarmed he's still homeless a year later.

"It's fine," he says. "I got his boat in a different bet, so we'll settle it soon."

Charlotte looks fascinated as she says, "The biggest thing I ever wagered was ten dollars on whether my husband could burp the tune to *Star*

Wars. You guys are really fearless about betting on homes and boats."

Dune laughs. "I'm a big fan of *Star Wars*. To quote Yoda... 'Fear is the path to the Dark Side. Fear leads to anger, anger leads to hate, hate leads to suffering.'"

Huh. That quote resonates with me. Yoda is wise. Perhaps that's why I'm languishing in anguish, because I'm subconsciously letting fear guide my decisions. Could it be that simple? I say I'm being brave and trying new things, but if I think about it, and admit it to myself, I'm always led by fear of the unknown in the end. I make a mental note to put *Star Wars* on the movie rotation.

Dune motions for us to sit. "Since there're three of you, I think that's a sign you're all going to get refunds."

"Let's hope," I say. Because I need a cash infusion. Whether it's for hiring an employee to help me from drowning in clay or for a down payment on an apartment in New Mexico, I cannot say.

"Last year filing solo!" Charlotte announces, taking a seat. "This time next year, I'll have a goddamn dependent. I always assumed I'd be claiming a dog, not a kid."

"Pregnant, huh?" Dune asks, dropping down into the executive leather chair, looking not at all like an accountant in his biker vest and tattoos. "Congratulations. Wish I could claim my baby on my taxes."

Speaking of Coco, she is still giving me withering death glares from the corner of the room as Dune spreads out tax forms and our folders we supplied. Wearing the bow I sent her, even. Ingrate. She saunters over to us and rubs her abundant white fur against Austin's leg.

"Hey, there...um...kitty?" Austin says.

Her round eyes bore into me as she pounces into Austin's lap, rubbing against his chest and nuzzling his chin with her snaggletoothed mouth. Oh my God. Is she...is she marking him as her territory as some sort of revenge against me?

"Huh, she never does that," Dune says, confirming my theory. "I'm usually the only man she loves on. Interesting she's acting like that with you."

Very.

Austin reaches out a hand, seems to think better of it and pulls it back, before ultimately giving in to pet her. She screeches lovingly and settles into his lap, pricking his jeans with her claws, taunting me.

"She seems to like you," I say, not taking my eyes off of her, lest she fly onto my face. "Didn't know you were good with cats."

"Cat people are a special breed." Dune turns to tap on the computer positioned at an angle on the desk. "Anyone can get a dog to like them, but a cat is more selective."

Austin whispers to me, "This is why I'm the pussy whisperer."

I've never heard Austin say the word *pussy* before and now I want to hear it again, a million times, over and over, but this is probably not the time or place. "You did not just say that."

He licks his lips. "Don't make me prove it."

My eyes are probably the size of Coco's as I stare back at him.

"Let's start with you, Austin," Dune says.

He asks him a question about a deduction and while they're deep in tax discussion, Charlotte texts me from the next seat over.

What's going on with you and Austin? He was very handsy outside and did I just hear him whisper the p-word?

In a stealth return text, I recap the whole entire situation for Charlotte, to which she sends at least twenty shocked emojis.

Chloe! What the?

I start typing my response, but it's a juggling routine since Dune is doing all three of us at once, so we're interrupted.

"Okay, Charlotte. What's this item?"

She leans forward to answer, and Austin whispers in my ear again, standing the hair at the nape of my neck on end. "You look pretty today."

A blush warms my face from his compliment just as Dune moves to my folder.

"I'm damn proud of you, Chloe." he says. "You even listed everything with a heading of All My Expenses. You killed it this year. And this spreadsheet you printed," he lets out a low whistle, "fucking phenomenal."

Austin's brows pull together as Dune continues to praise me. "Thank you. You taught me everything I know about spreadsheets."

He looks up at me, piercing me with a stare. "That I did. If you need a refresher course, just let me know."

From my peripheral, I see Austin scrub a hand along his jaw. He shifts forward a bit. "I've helped her log the numbers. She's good."

"Yeah?" Dune says, tapping a pen on the desk. "You sure about that?"

Austin doesn't flinch beneath Dune's stern gaze. "Yeah. Why would you think she's not?"

My phone vibrates and I peek at it.

We are literally sitting in the office of the PRESIDENT of a motorcycle GANG. Baby Charlotte-to-be would like to be born. Make them stop.

"Thank you, both," I say with a wan smile, in an attempt to defuse things before it turns into a real *Motorcycle Mayhem 4: All's Fair in Bikes and War* situation. "I think I'm comfortable with spreadsheets."

Dune returns to accountant mode, and while he and Austin put aside their alpha to discuss a receipt, I text Charlotte.

Is Austin jealous of Dune?

Ya think? I'd say his jealousy is as obvious as your nipples when Austin wiped that ketchup off your chin earlier.

Stahp! You could've told me I was drooling ketchup!

You stop!

Dune interrupts us to have Charlotte fill in some missing information on a form. While they're busy, Austin whispers in my ear again. This time, ghosting his lips against the sensitive skin as he says. "Are you guys texting about me? Do you need to Porch?"

He says the last part loud enough for Dune to hear.

"Everything okay?" Dune asks. "You're not hiding income, are you? I've got a special form for that if—"

"Haha, no," I say. "It's lady talk. We're just going to the bathroom. Charlotte pees so much now." I nudge Charlotte when she completes her form requirements.

"Yep, I pee every three minutes," she says, standing. "Come with me for lady talk, please, Chloe."

Dune gives us directions and in the bathroom, I tell her Austin asked me out on a real date, but I haven't accepted and needed to think about how I should answer. Because I'm an adult who doesn't make rash decisions. In my next life, I will be, anyway.

She blinks. "Seriously? Like a couple date?"

"Yes."

"Do you want to go on a date with him?"

"I don't know! I mean, yeah, I told him to ask me on a date, so obviously I do, but should I?"

"What's the should? If you want to, you do it."

"Because I'm dating Logan."

She clasps my shoulders and turns me toward a cool leather chair in the corner of the room. "Sit and prepare yourself. I'm going to practice parenting with you."

"Oh, okay. Good idea."

"Ahem. You need to grow up." I open my mouth, stung that she thinks I'm acting like a child when I'm trying so hard to be mature, but she cuts me off with a raised finger. "Nope, I'm still going. This is silly and you know it. We're gossiping about boys in a bathroom."

"You're right. I know you are. Granny Mae says I should date them both, but there really wasn't a good time to tell Logan about that last night."

"She's a wise woman. Look—Austin knows about Logan. You need to tell Logan if you're going to go on a date with Austin. People do this all the time. It's not like you're the first. And frankly, seeing as you and Logan are not official, I'm also going to pull the feminist card and say we wouldn't even be having this conversation if you were a man. You aren't doing anything wrong. You just need to decide what you want, and then communicate it to everyone." She gives me a pointed look. "Like an adult."

"You're going to be the best mom ever."

"I'm seeing myself more as the dad…"

"Okay, I didn't want to be the one to say it, but yeah. Best daddy ever."

We hug and return to find Dune showing Austin some of his recent ink. "Hey, Chloe, check this out," he says, and holds out his arm.

I close the space between us and there on his wrist is… "Is that an inch line?"

"Yep. It reminds me to be more present. You taught me that."

"Very cool. I'm glad I inspired you."

Austin clears his throat, and Dune glances between us. "You did. And even if you're not my woman, you'll always be family." He stares at Austin. "You've got her back when I'm not around?"

"I've got her back even when I'm not around," Austin says, setting a swoon swarm alight in my belly. "She's good."

"I believe you, brother," Dune says.

"Good. Because I don't say things I don't mean. Especially when it comes to Chloe."

Dang. I rub my own inch line.

And it reminds me that I do know who I am now, and that I can ask for what I want.

"Well, this has been the most interesting tax filing ever," Charlotte says. "I'm going to recommend you to all my friends."

Dune grins, and the tension in the air lifts. We decide to break for dessert and head into the backyard. After chocolate cake and apple pie, Dune takes Austin to scope out the bikes and Charlotte and I mingle with the guests. The women make plans to send Baby Charlotte to-be biker onesies, and I like being part of this family. Once our taxes are finished, and we say goodbye, and also snag some to-go plates, I tell Austin I'll go out with him.

But first...I need to talk to Logan.

NINE

LIFE IS MY BITCH. The board game, that is, but I'll take it since my real life didn't come with easy-to-follow directions.

Austin and I are having a "not-a-date" night at home, because I decided I should have an important conversation like the one I need to have with Logan in person, and it'll be a while.

Austin respected my decision to wait until I talk to Logan, but he also insisted that after a week's worth of twelve-hour days schlepping clay back and forth from the store's kiln I needed a break. So instead of a real date outside of these walls he made fresh, fried potato chips and his signature French onion dip, while I uncorked a bottle of Merlot and dug out my white elephant gift from the work

Christmas party—The Game of Life: Quarter Life Crisis.

"No way," Austin mutters as he lands on a spot to downgrade his job. "I'm screwed."

"Bummer," I say with a grin and pop a chip into my mouth. "Your bad luck streak continues."

This parody version of the original is much more authentic to real life. Not only do you start with no money, you also get crushed with a staggering $500,000 in debt to pay off to win. Like the original, to start the game, you have a tiny plastic car, but you are randomly given a job for income and a house to rent, along with a side hustle to help you erase your debt.

Fun, right? In the real world, this is what happens so you can afford to have furniture you don't put together yourself while surviving solely on ramen noodles.

"This isn't life." He frowns. "Whoever made this game needs to reassess their living skills."

He says that because he's losing.

"What's more lifelike than getting divorced, paying more than you can afford for childcare, and changing jobs?"

He holds his card up. "Why would I choose to go from making $60k as a waiter to only $40k making cheese?"

I laugh. "It's the hipster way. Besides, I'll have you know that someone gave Queen Victoria a giant wheel of cheddar cheese that weighed over 1,000 pounds as a wedding gift. If it's good enough for the Queen, it's certainly a respectable job for you."

"Pfft. I think I like the original game better," he grumbles.

"Don't hate the game, hate the player," I tease.

I say that because I'm winning.

"I could never hate you," he volleys back in a husky tone that sends my pulse racing through my veins. "Even if you're kicking my ass."

I am so kicking his ass. In this game of life, although twice divorced, the game gods have blessed me with good luck. My debt-to-income ratio is phenomenal.

To recap—

Me:
Occupation: Assistant to the Assistant Manager, $40,000 annually
House: Tree House, Rent: $20,000 a year
Side hustle: Podcast Host

Austin:

(New) Occupation: Artisanal Cheesemaker, Salary: $40,000 annually
House: Starter Home, Rent: $40,000 a year
Side hustle: Alpaca Farmer

We continue on life's twisted path, and Austin's side hustle is the only thing keeping him afloat. Besides his astonishing good looks, obviously.

"Pay up," I say when he spins a three, which is the designated number for me to get paid $20,000 for my side gig. "Ah, it feels good that I'm getting closer to climbing out of my debt."

I make a gimme signal with my hand, which he ignores. Instead of giving me my payday, he makes love to his bottom lip with the pad of his thumb, caressing it across the slight swell of it, dark eyes studying me from under lids stationed at half-mast. "I have a proposition for you. How about we make a trade?"

"What kind of trade?" If he says sex, I am *not* strong enough to resist.

"I'll be a guest on your show and tell your viewers all about the many wonders of cheese. I'll make cheese sexy again."

If anyone can do it, he can.

"I must have missed its sexy phase."

"Cheese can be very sexy." So can he. "It can be hard or soft. It melts and stretches—"

I squirm in my spot on the floor and shake my head to disperse the dirty thoughts. "That's tempting, and thank you for your generosity, but nope."

"How about a snuggly pair of socks, spun from the softest alpaca hair on earth?"

"Softest on earth, huh?" I take a sip of wine. "That's a mighty big claim."

His brow arches with innuendo. "It is big."

Throughout the game, he's flirted and twice, I've wanted to shove the board off the table and pounce on him. It's overwhelming and heady to be the object of his desire.

"Hm." I do love socks...and also the way he's looking at me right now with his eyes full of sexual promises I want to see if he can keep. "Again, it's tempting, but I'm raising five kids in my treehouse, and just got divorced again so I don't know if mommy needs a new pair of alpaca socks."

"I'll make all the babies pairs too. And furry coats to keep their tiny plastic bodies warm." To tempt me further, he reaches beneath the coffee table where we sit on opposite sides, and whispers his fingertips along my bare foot. "You can come over to my starter home...the kids can play with the alpacas, and I'll slip them on you myself."

"I'm not sure that's allowed. What if they spit on the babies?"

"We can make our own rules. While you're enjoying your new foot-huggers, I'll even give you the moon"—my heart lurches against my chest that he remembers our conversation from so long ago—"made from the very best cheese."

Damn. I don't even care if it's made from clabbered milk; I want the moon.

"Okay."

Even though I have accepted his bribe, he continues to massage my foot, working his thumb along the sole to the heel until I can barely think straight.

"Did you know Milton Bradley created the game to teach children about ethics?" I say as Austin thumps the spinner, sending it whirring in a circle.

"Interesting. I didn't know that. I figured it was to teach you that money is the answer to all your problems."

"If only," I say. Not that I have enough of it to test the theory.

He finally removes his hand from my foot to drive his purple car along the path and lands on a spot where he must choose whether to get married.

"Yeah," he says without hesitation. "I want a wife."

He says it with such conviction, my hand trembles as I hand him his tiny plastic bride. "Congratulations. May all your days be joyous."

As he places the pink peg in the seat beside him, I can't help but imagine it's me.

"Wait," he says, "we can't marry each other?"

Oh God, he's mind-reading. I nearly choke on my chip, but thankfully it saves me from blurting out *yes*.

"You okay?"

I nod and reach for my glass of wine to guzzle a large gulp before taking my turn.

"Yasss," I say when I land on a space to upgrade my job to a pro-gamer, doubling my income.

"Now you're just rubbing your superiority in my face," he says.

Oh, how I'd love to rub things *on* his face. But I can't. I won't. Not until I talk to Logan.

Austin finally hits the baby space, and this is where life really takes a u-turn.

"You should hope for one child," I say, "because I don't know if you can afford more than that."

When you land on the babies spot for the first time, you spin the wheel to see how many you'll get, but if you stop on that space again, you have to pay $20,000 per kid for daycare.

"I want at least three."

"I thought you didn't want any kids at all?"

"I didn't want kids with Lucy." He dazzles me with an earnest grin. "The future looks different now that I have a pink peg."

His words are all I think about as I finally win the game. Now, if I could just win in my real life.

LIFE IS REALLY JUST a series of events that happen to you. One day, I'll learn not to over-prepare and overthink situations.

"I'm more of a people person," Dominic says on our Zoom call, rendering all of my preparation for this interview useless. "So, I don't follow the traditional interview route."

I'd already guessed that based on the virtual mountainous background with horses surrounding his mustached dark head. It's like he's in the Wild West and may challenge me to a duel at any moment.

"I like people too," I say, which may or may not be true, but seems an appropriate response.

"I'm going to do something off the cuff to get a feel for you. Let me see what background you choose. Take a few minutes and select what you think fits your personality best."

Well, this is awkward. "Oh, ha. I've already selected a background." The neat room behind me isn't mine. "I kind of liked the furniture and art in this one."

He laughs. "I like it. So tell me...what would the title of your autobiography be?"

"Throwing Rocks: A Memoir of My Many Mistakes," I answer on the fly.

"Huh. I'd read that."

"Thanks. It would be a bestseller, I'm sure."

"What's your favorite monkey?"

"I don't have one," I fib. Orangutans are my favorite but I won't fall into his interview trap.

"That would be the only correct answer," he says.

We continue on for another five minutes with him asking absurd questions that make me wonder if I could actually work for this man.

After I give him an answer that I would be a refrigerator if I were a kitchen appliance, he leans back in his chair. "I'd like to offer you the job."

I should be more excited than I am, but I feign a squeal and express my gratitude.

"I'll email you an offer letter by next week and you'll have some time to look over it and sign it. My assistant Carley will give you all the details."

I thank him again, and after we disconnect I stare at the blank screen. Be careful what you wish for, because you just might get it. I may move to Santa

Fe. Everything is falling into place, yet falling apart. And I need to figure out the loose ends before I unravel completely. I pick up my phone and FaceTime Logan.

He answers on the second ring. "Hey, you."

"Hi. I got the job in Santa Fe."

"Wow." He pauses, and something is off with his grin. It's pained? "Congratulations. So you're moving to Santa Fe?"

"I'm not sure." I dive headfirst into the murky waters. "What is the status of our relationship?"

"What do you mean?"

"Well, I'm just not sure how to define us."

He's silent for a moment and then blows out a breath. "I know I haven't pushed for the traditional relationship labels, but I didn't think I needed to."

"I'm just not sure about the future," I tell him. "Or what you see for the future."

"I want the whole she-bang. I'm a selfish bastard and don't want you to go to Santa Fe. I want to live with you and wake up to you and I've realized, being without you, how much I like you being there."

Speechless, I stare at his handsome face. Everything he said is everything I could possibly want to hear. It's romantic. It's secure. It's what I wondered, at Charlotte's wedding, if anyone would ever say to me. But...there will always be a "but" until I get Austin out of my system.

"I'm not there yet," I say with regret. God, I wish I was there. "This is the first year I've really tried dating, and even though I really thought I had myself figured out, I haven't. If I need a little more time to decide, would you hate me?"

His heavy sigh makes my chest ache. "No. Put this on hold. We'll keep it non-exclusive until I get back from the tour, and we can talk about it then."

"So you wouldn't be mad if I go on a date tomorrow night with someone?"

"I don't want to hear about it, but if that's what you need to do..."

It is. There's no way I can not get this out of my system. It's not fair to Logan to not have my whole heart available.

Date night with Austin is a go.

TEN

HEEL OR WEDGE is the first world problem of the day. I FaceTime Charlotte wearing one of each to help me choose a shoe for my date with Austin.

"Tan wedge," she replies. "Dang. You look gorgeous! The loose curls and hints of makeup are perfect with that dress."

"You're such a wonderful critique partner."

Over the years, we've come to an understanding not to give a generic compliment and save time by analyzing the entire look from top to bottom.

"It's true. That outfit was worth every penny," she praises.

If only it were pennies. The floaty wrap dress that stops mid-thigh is now the priciest item of clothing I own, but a justified purchase in my mind. Austin and I already know most everything about each other so technically I could wear pajamas, but If I'm going to risk our friendship, and my budding relationship with Logan, might as well go all in and look my best for our date. Most important, I've got matching black undergarments beneath the dusty pink floral dress covering them.

"Wish I could be there when he sees the effort you put into making him feel valued."

"Well...dating experts agree it's important to nail a first impression. But hello. It's tricky to achieve that when you've already had your first impression. We've plateaued and haven't even left yet."

"Who are these experts, Eeyore?"

"VIIPs...Very Important Internet People."

"Stop! You will definitely impress him. He's not seen what's under that dress."

This is true, so there's still hope I can dazzle him with my sleek vagina. At Charlotte's nudging, we had a spa day and got ourselves waxed. I was a little reluctant after the last ladyscaping fiasco, but gave in when she broke down in sobs and said she wouldn't be able to see hers soon so I must take one for the team.

So, I did.

To be clear, I don't plan on flashing him my privates, but as Charlotte pointed out, one never knows if the breeze will lift one's skirt so it's best to be prepared if a wind sweeps through Boulder and rips one's panties off. Which is the same logic I used before so the possibility of it happening might not be zero. It does get pretty windy.

"You know I'm semi-neurotic, so tell me again I'm not making a mistake."

"You're not," she replies to my incessant worry. "There's more to lose if you don't do this. Girl. Stop leaping ahead and fixating on potential problems that may never materialize. He values your friendship just as much and he's forging ahead anyway, so it's not like you're in this alone. Besides, everyone knows I'd kill you both if you screwed this up."

That's what I needed to hear to calm the fears in my head. Besides, the internet gurus say that in the case of dating a friend, worrying about the outcome of your friendship in every phase of your romantic development is not recommended. I've done extensive research on first dates and have reached the conclusion that I'll never do everything perfectly. It's best to forgo the dating advice and rely on instinct to get me through tonight.

"Thank you for your advice! Part of me still can't believe we're going on a date. It's surreal."

A year ago, when I signed up for FriendsOfFriends to get over my crush, I never would've guessed life would take me right back. But after all the fantasies of what there could be between us, I can't help but wonder—what if?

What if, after all this time spent pining for him, my date with Austin is a letdown?

It's a valid concern and entirely possible. When you're atop a pedestal as high as the one I put him on, is there anywhere to go but down? As I have learned the hard way, chemistry can only get you so far in a relationship. There are so many things I need answers to.

We're attracted to each other, but do we have parallel life plans?

Do I even know what my life plan is, with the offer letter sitting on my computer?

Do we have what it takes to have a healthy partnership?

If we date, are we also living together?

What do you call a question with no answer?

I'm in a holding pattern. Yes, being friends is a huge thing out of the way, but a romantic relationship is complex and how do I know that he'll be able to handle things like—I need my ears to be covered to sleep?

"Five more minutes," Charlotte texts. "Have fun. Can't wait for brunch tomorrow to get all the deets!"

Her countdown to the agreed upon time for us to

leave makes my palms sweat. I say goodbye and quickly tuck my phone into my bag.

As I slip on the other caramel-colored wedge, the doorbell quacks. I freeze. Please, don't let this be something or someone to ruin tonight.

It quacks again. And again.

Austin is nowhere to be seen as I exit my bedroom and cross the living room to the door.

My breath catches when I open it to find Austin, dressed in slacks paired with a black button-down, dark hair perfectly rumpled, holding a daisy plucked from our flourishing garden.

"Fuck," he murmurs, sweeping his gaze over my body. "You look…beautiful." He hands me the flower.

"What are you doing out here?"

"Since we live together, it's a little hard to pick you up, but I wanted to experience that with you. So, hi."

"Austin," I whisper. "That's so sweet."

He's a great dater, and my heart agrees, thrashing and pounding against my chest, wanting to live in his hand.

"I'd invite you in, but my roommate…"

"Great guy, I've heard."

"The best." I tuck the delicate flower behind my ear and hurry back inside to grab my handbag. "Ready?"

"Yeah," he says. "I'm ready."

A warm hand lands on the small of my back and guides me to his Subaru. He opens the door and I climb inside...as his date.

His date.

I am going on a date with Austin!

He rounds the hood and hops in, overwhelming my senses with his clean, woodsy scent.

"Where are we going?" I ask as he backs out of the driveway.

"It's a surprise."

"It's not your parents' house, is it?"

He laughs and rests his forearm on the console, and *places his hand on my thigh*. "No. And I'm not going to make you bowl or climb a mountain."

"Sounds like the best date ever."

So far, it is. As he drives us toward the twinkling lights of downtown, it's natural and filled with easy conversation. Thank God he can't hear the constant internal squeals in my head when he does simple things like look over at me and lick his lips. We agreed we can't talk about the L's and I do my best not to think about them for this one night.

When we arrive, he navigates into a parking garage.

"So, what are we doing?" I ask as we walk toward the street.

"I figured if you're going to be in the art world, I need to know more about it. So, First Friday for our first date. A night of firsts."

"Really?" I nearly squeal with excitement.

It's so perfect and so...romantic.

Within ten minutes, hand in hand, we're immersed in the arts district along Broadway. Studios and art galleries taking part can be found by hand-painted signs, and I don't think the smile leaves my face as we tour them all. We meet painters, sculptors, and other artists, and not once does Austin lose interest. He asks questions and studies the wares, all while finding time to trail a hand down my back or put his arm around my shoulders.

It's everything I could've imagined.

Live music serenades us as we wander down the street after a delicious dinner at an Italian bistro.

"You could have your own restaurant like that," I say as we amble closer to the parking garage.

"I've fantasized about that," he says. "Opening a tiny Italian place." He looks down at me as we near the Subaru. "Where you make all the serving dishes. Of course, that's not likely to happen if you go to Santa Fe."

The fact he would want to use my products in his dream restaurant is beyond words. "Maybe we add Santa Fe to the off-limits talk list?"

"Actually, that's a good segue. I wanted to tell you..." He opens the door for me, and on the drive home tells me the owner of the restaurant he works for is retiring next year, and he wants to train him to take over, possibly sell it to him.

"Wow. Austin, that's an awesome opportunity. I'm so happy for you."

"Yeah. I'd have to get some big loans and dip into my savings but it's worth it."

"Definitely."

The rest of the ride we talk about what he'd change in the restaurant, new menu items, and before I know it, we're home. Our date is over.

I'm thankful for the cloak of darkness in the car when he cuts the engine and turns to me to say in a low voice, "You know, you were the inspiration for me saying yes."

His declaration hits me right in the feels. "That's the nicest compliment anyone has ever given me. And this has been the best date ever."

"This is the part where I walk you to the door and say good night."

On the way there, my feet don't touch the ground. It's like I'm floating in a dream. And I do not want to wake up, because on the porch, with the breeze tugging his hair, and the moon watching us, he cups my face and pulls me in for a hungry kiss that raises his pedestal higher than the stars.

Our moans mingle in the cool air as his hand glides up my thigh, beneath my skirt, leaving a wildfire in its wake. Heat sears my skin, seeps in my pores, and blazes my insides.

From just a touch.

My back hits the wall of the house with a thud as he breaks the kiss to suck a path along my neck, while his roaming fingers inch closer to the ache between my legs.

"You have no idea how many times I imagined doing this. How often I've jerked off thinking about you." I groan as his touch teases me. The pad of his thumb presses down on the throbbing bundle of nerves in my clit. "I've imagined what you'd sound like moaning. What you'd look like coming. Have you ever thought about me and touched yourself?"

"Yes," I admit, panting. "Many times."

His thumb presses harder, and he adds a knee to the mix so I can grind on it. "Someday, you're going to do it and let me watch. Would you let me watch?"

"Only if I can watch you too."

He leans in for another kiss, nipping my lips, claiming my mouth, and the sensations in my body build until the cataclysmic explosion can no longer be contained.

"I'm going to come," I say.

He groans, his body bucking into mine, and palms my pussy, rubbing his hand back and forth in a frenzy, creating enough friction to blow my mind with my first ever over-the-panties orgasm.

Warmth spreads through my body, and tingles dance across my skin in a pirouette of pleasure. My back arches and I can't hold back the long moan that escapes me as I come hard on his hand.

"Jesus," he murmurs as I soar toward heaven.

When I finally drift back to earth, the bulge in his pants looks painful.

"Should I, um...are you..."

He kisses my forehead, cheeks, and lips. "I want to take it slow. When I'm inside of you, I don't want any other man near your mind."

"Thank you for everything," I whisper, because I can barely talk. "It was amazing."

He smirks. "We're just getting started. I've got a lot more to give you."

We head inside and go our separate ways to bed. He says he'll wait for the third date for more.

But as I lie in mine alone, I don't know if I'll make it that far.

ELEVEN

"IF YOU MOVE to Santa Fe, can I come with you?" Charlotte asks over the mountain of dry toast heaped on her plate. "I think I'd thrive in a drier climate."

We met up for brunch for our planned after-date recap, but that's been put aside because the spider senses I gained last spring in my outing with Finn tell me Charlotte's in desperate need of some impromptu therapy since she didn't want kids and now she's preggo.

"I don't know if Mr. Charlotte will be okay with you moving away. And your skin looks amazing. You're practically glowing."

"It's because I'm sweating," she says. "I'm having hot flashes or something. And honestly, I don't care what he's okay with anymore. He can visit or write me letters. Serves him right for knocking me up on our honeymoon, like a Victorian couple."

"Are you all right? Tell me your troubles."

She leans in with sad brown eyes focused on me and whispers, "I'm going to say something utterly selfish, and we can chalk it up to the raging hormones that are holding my body hostage. Okay?"

"Okay."

"No judgment?"

"None."

"I don't want you to go, Chloe. I want you to turn it down, even though it's your dream job. I don't care that it's more money and what you've always wanted. I want you to stay here in Colorado with me. Because I need help to survive this pregnancy and motherhood thing, and I won't survive without you." She leans back. "Now you say something selfish, so I don't feel so bad."

"I want to be you. But not in a *Hand That Rocks the Cradle* way. I want a loving husband and the kids and the cute little bump in my belly. I want to take all of you to Santa Fe with me, and uproot you from your happy life here, so I won't be alone. Santa Fe is only six hours away, but it feels like six hundred. It feels way too far."

Tears shimmer in her eyes. "Oh God, I'm going to cry."

"Don't cry," I plead, fighting back tears of my own. "If I go, we'll still see each other regularly. I'll come up on weekends as often as I can. You can come visit me too." She wipes her eyes. "Please, don't cry."

"It's unstoppable. I cry over everything now. The other day, I burnt my pizza and bawled for thirty minutes. And I didn't even want pizza!" I listen as she gets everything off her burgeoning chest. "My worst moment was in the grocery store when the guy in the bakery told me they were out of chocolate croissants and I started blubbering in front of ten people. I don't enjoy being a crier. Other Mother said to get used to it, that this baby will give me cause to weep an ocean. And I cried over that too."

"Well, I have no experience in this area, but I've heard people say this stuff is all temporary. Maybe you can take a class?"

"For crying?"

I laugh. "No. A parenting class."

"Maybe." She sighs. "I don't really want you to turn down that opportunity. But I do want to go with you."

"Charlotte," I say gently, fighting back tears of my own, "it's going to be okay."

"You don't understand. It's the weirdest thing ever that's going on within my body. I have super-smelling abilities now. Like a bloodhound. Think I'm exaggerating? Someone is pouring syrup right now, aren't they?"

I glance over to the diners seated next to us and spy a lady four tables behind us lathering her stack of pancakes in gooey syrup.

"Huh. Yep, they are. That's pretty cool." I smile, but she doesn't.

"It's not cool at all. I can smell it all the way over here, and if they don't stop, I might gag. I've always loved syrup, but now, it's revolting." She picks up a triangle of toast. "You think I want this dry? I don't. I want it smothered in butter and jam, but the nugget inside me says no."

"It'll pass," I reassure her. "I'm sure you'll like things you hated before too. My mom always tells a story about how she never liked ranch dressing until she was pregnant with me."

She shivers. "Yuck. Just the thought of that makes me want to hurl."

"Okay, listen. Push all those thoughts away and think of all the tiny cuteness swaddled next to your bosom."

"But what if I don't like swaddling? Or things touching my bosom? Or...what if I just don't like the kid? You can't order the one you want, you just get what you get and maybe I get one that is incompatible with me. Can I just give it to you? I think I'd make a really cool aunt."

"You'll make a really cool mom, too," I insist. "And I hear you tend to like your own."

Charlotte isn't convinced, and before I can say anything further, a shadow falls on our table. I glance up to see not our waiter...but Austin.

"What are you doing here?"

"I figured it was your after-date recap, and I wasn't going to miss that." He motions for me to scoot over in the booth.

"But you can't...when you were the date..."

He slides in next to me. "Why not?"

Charlotte thinks it's a great idea for him to take part, which I suspect is because she really isn't interested in therapizing herself further and could use the backup.

"It's healthy to have a discussion where both people can provide feedback," she coaxes. "And I need the distraction from my problems."

"I don't know," I say.

"Come on, Chloe," Austin says. "You won't even know I'm here."

"Please?" Charlotte gives me puppy-dog eyes.

"Oh, all right." Because I'm a good friend, I try to pretend Austin isn't here as I open up to Charlotte. "It was an amazing date."

"How so?" Austin asks. "What was your favorite part? Beginning, middle...or end?"

My eyes widen at the memory of the spectacular orgasm on the porch, and I give his leg a swift nudge with my foot under the table, then swing back to caress it.

"Let her finish," Charlotte says. "I need all the swoony details."

I twist my napkin between my fingers. "You know how much I've liked Austin. And how deeply I feel about him because of how well he knows me." She nods. "And our friendship is so amazing. You said living with him would be a bad idea, but—"

"You said living with me would be a bad idea?" Austin interjects, glaring at Charlotte.

I defend her. "She did, but she was right to say that. Because I already liked you so much, and she was afraid I couldn't get over you if I was with you all the time, and she was right about that too."

"See, I'm smart," Charlotte says with a smile.

"So you think living with me is a bad idea?" Austin huffs.

"No. Despite all that, I also wouldn't trade this time with you for anything, because I love being your roommate. And I love..." I catch myself before I say anything too honest. "Your sandwiches. But"—I look away from him—"Logan is the best relationship

I've ever had. I don't want to just throw that away, and I don't want to screw up my friendship with you."

Austin tilts my face back to him with a finger under the chin. "I don't want to screw up our friendship either," he insists. "It's the most important thing to me."

"I think you have this," Charlotte says. "I'm going to step outside and make a phone call. Then I'll be in the restroom for a while, doing pregnant woman things." She stands and leaves us to talk alone.

Austin shifts to face me. "Why is he the best relationship? And how do you know we won't be better?"

I love that I can talk about Logan and being confused with Austin without fear of reprisal. "Well, he likes my sense of humor—"

"So do I."

"He's a good guy, and he's dependable."

"So am I. You're really not giving me anything here about what makes him the better choice. Other than that, he doesn't have the stigma of being your good friend attached to him. Doesn't seem that serious to me."

"I'm not minimizing my connection with you, but I have feelings for him." His jaw ticks. "And if you hadn't broken up with Lucy, I probably would have moved in with him," I reveal.

"And it would've been a mistake," he says matter-of-factly.

"Why?"

"Because even with all those feelings, you still went out with me."

"You had opportunities to make a move on me before. You obviously didn't think it was cool to feel things out with me while still with Lucy. Now you're asking me to do that for you."

"Lucy and I were more serious," Austin interjects. "It's not the same."

"Maybe it's not exactly the same, but it still feels like you could have stepped up before, and now that you've decided you want me, I should automatically follow your timeline. Maybe you only like me because I'm taken."

"It's not the only reason I like you." He scoots closer and lowers his voice. "I'm going to be honest, Chloe. I didn't like you going out with all those guys. Do you know why?"

"Why?"

"Because they weren't me." He takes the napkin from my hand and threads his fingers in its place. "At first, I figured it was something you needed to do to grow, but then I got scared you'd outgrow me. And that's when I realized I was fighting more than an attraction to a friend. And I didn't want to lose you either." His dark eyes bore into mine. "Obviously, I don't know what the future holds. There's a chance you may find that I'm not worthy of you. And you'd probably be right."

It ends up being an actual open and honest conversation where we put all our fears on the table that's still loaded with our half-eaten brunch and we talk about all the things that could go wrong.

"What if things start to break down and it's so awkward we can't be in social settings together? I can't give up Charlotte's baby-to-be, and if you avoid going to things because of me, I'll feel guilty that I'm keeping you from going. See? It's already a mess—"

His lips cut my words off. His hand clasps the back of my neck as his mouth brushes across mine, and all the incessant worries vanish.

He pulls away. "Did you feel that?"

"Yeah," I murmur.

"That's really all I have to say. What you decide and who you choose is up to you. Just remember everything could also go really right between us."

And that's why I decide to accept a second date if he offers.

And he does.

Charlotte returns and Austin leaves us to finish our recap. We watch him navigate through the tables and once his tall frame is out of sight, Charlotte wastes no time begging me to fill her in on everything that happened while she was gone. I do, and by the time I'm finished, she's as torn over the situation as I am.

"I love Austin," she says. "And now that some time has passed since Lucy, I think you'd be great together. But I also think you'd be great with Logan. It's a tough decision, and just because you already know Austin and know you can trust him, doesn't mean he's the right choice."

I blow out a breath. "Yeah."

We finish our meal, and when it's time to pay, our server informs us that Austin already took care of it. She places two to-go boxes on the table. "He said to add a slice of our homemade chocolate cake for both of you."

"Well, I think Austin just threw down the gauntlet," Charlotte says. "I'm always open to bribery with chocolate cake. I'm glad I don't have to choose between them."

"Wish I didn't either," I say. "This is an impossible decision."

We say goodbye in the parking lot, and when I get in my car, I receive a text that just may be the deciding factor.

Meet me for coffee in the morning?

TWELVE

WHO DECIDED to let me be an adult? Seriously, it's in the world's best interest to have people fill out an application for adulthood approval. If that were the case, though, I'm sure what I'm about to do would cause my request to be denied. And I think I'd be okay with that decision. Adulting is hard.

Aromatic coffee punches me in the nose when I open the door to Brewhaha, a local coffee shop. Even though it's barely eight a.m., there is already a line of sluggish customers waiting for a shot of roasted beans to wake them up so they can pretend to be adults. *I know*, I want to tell them. *I know the secret. We're all faking it.*

In the cafe's back corner, I spot my early morning coffee date, dark hair glowing in the shafts of sunlight streaming in the window, looking more chipper and put together than everyone else in the place.

"Hi," Lucy says when I reach the table. "Thanks for meeting me so early on a Sunday."

"Hey. No problem." I take a seat across from her, wondering if an adultier adult would have agreed to this meeting. "How are you?"

"I'm doing fantastic." She says it like she means it, and since she picked such a strong word, I believe it's true, which is rather surprising to me. "I ordered you a caramel cappuccino to save time. Hope you don't mind." She pushes the paper cup toward me with pink-tipped nails that match her off-the-shoulder shirt. "I remember once upon a time Austin picked that up for you on our way to his house, so hope you still like it."

"Thank you." Is it bad I'm wondering if it's poisoned? "Yes, it's my favorite."

She takes a sip of whatever is in her cup, and eyes me over the rim. Dread churns in my stomach while I blow on the hot liquid in my hand and wait for her to tell me why she wanted to talk today. When I responded and asked what was up, she vaguely said it was "something important," so I have no idea if this is a confrontation or a plea for me to help her get Austin back.

Neither option is appealing.

The fact that I'm sitting across from her golden shoulders is a testament to my growth. In the past I would have rather done a hundred burpees than face her, but I guess I *am* growing up. Getting up at the crack of dawn while Austin still slept and sneaking out to meet her seemed like the right thing to do. Well. It did until I thought of it like that.

"So, what did you want to talk about?" I prod when she doesn't divulge the reason we're here.

"Oh, yes. Well, I just wanted to do this face-to-face." She sets her cup down, still a master at prolonging the agony. "I could've done this over the phone, but I felt we needed to do this in person."

Dear God, is she about to tell me we need to see other people?

"You're killing me here," I say. "Put me out of my misery?"

She laughs and rests her elbows on the table. "Okay, so...I need your help."

Oh, no. She wants Austin back, and this is about to get really awkward. "With what?"

"You're never going to believe this. Never in a million years."

"Just tell me."

"So, you know when I said I had a date the day I picked up the box?"

"Yes, I remember."

"Well, it was with Finn."

My head snaps back. "What? I saw him last fall, and I thought he was engaged?"

She rolls her eyes. "He was, but it didn't last long. I guess she broke it off with him, because she couldn't handle the healthy lifestyle."

"Ah. And what do you need my help with?"

"I just wanted some insider information. I'm meeting the parents next weekend, and I like to be prepared." She trails a nail around the rim of her cup. "I know you met them before your breakup. Austin didn't really tell me what happened other than you broke up, but I figured it must've not gone well and I want to avoid the same mistakes."

This is a lot to digest, and so not what I expected. "So you two are serious?"

She shrugs. "We've just really clicked with all the time we spent together working on the PR for Super-Fit. And we have great workouts together, and now we're both bonding over our breakups."

"I won't lie and say I'm not shocked. But it makes a certain amount of sense." A large amount, actually. "I'm glad you're happy."

She studies me for a moment. "I know Austin has a thing for you. He told me."

"Oh."

"It's okay. I'm not the type to dwell on those sorts

of things. I'm a forward-facing woman, and honestly, I think Finn better suits me and my goals. Isn't it funny how things work out for the better?"

She goes on to tell me the long version of the story about how she tried to fight her feelings for Finn while she was away all that time doing SuperFit things, trying desperately to convince herself that moving in was what would fix things, but when Austin broke up with her after catching the bouquet at Charlotte's wedding, she felt it was a sign straight from the heavens. I can't do anything but listen with fascination that she's so enamored with someone I found to be so self-centered. Different strokes, I guess?

"So help a girl out? Share your secrets."

Lucy may have been my nemesis, but she also attempted to help me in her own way, so now it's my turn to return the favor. "Do you bowl?"

She tilts her head. "No, why?"

"Did he tell you about his family?"

"Not a lot. Just that he thinks his dad will love me but his stepmom is a tougher sell."

Well, at least he forewarned her about Stepmommy Dearest. As my final atonement, I gift her my knowledge about Finn and his family. Her mouth falls open when I get to the breakup.

"He's the heir to the SuperFit gyms?"

I nod. "Yep."

"I can understand why they have to protect their fortune. Must be so hard to weed out the gold diggers." I guess that's one way to look at it. "Not to brag, but I'm athletically inclined so I don't think there will be any issues there."

"It's been a year since I bowled myself into a breakup with him, so who knows, maybe they've moved onto a new test."

Instead of being horrified, she's intrigued and starry-eyed. "I love challenges. I can't thank you enough for the tip-off." She picks up her purse. "Sorry to run off, but I'm meeting Finn to look at properties. He's in this godawful tiny house, and I just can't handle it."

She gives me a half-hug and flounces away, and on the drive home, my shoulders feel a bit lighter that I got that closure with my guilt over her. And that she had her own closure, whether with the weird one-sided friendship with me or with her sign from the universe about Austin. Regardless, I think her insular kind of affection may have found it's own tiny—er, giant home in Finn's life.

When I arrive home, the house is filled with the scrumptious scent of blueberries. I find Austin in the kitchen, whisking something in a stainless steel bowl.

"Hope you're hungry," he says. "I made pancakes with homemade whipped cream."

"Starved," I say. Interesting choice of flavors, too.

He runs his finger along the whisk, collecting the yummy goodness from the metal, and holds it out to me. "Tell me how it tastes."

Not one to turn down his offering, I move closer and suck his finger into my mouth.

"Oops," he says, watching me. "That was probably a mistake on my part, because now I want to feed you the whole bowl with my fingers."

The truth is, I'd let him, but I step away. "It's delicious."

Out of the corner of my eye, I see him adjust himself before he dollops the cream on top of pancakes drizzled with blueberry compote.

We move to the table with our plates, and once we're seated he says, "I've been thinking, and there's one thing we didn't discuss yesterday—your career."

"Yeah." I push my fork through the blueberries.

"What do you want to do?"

"I don't know anymore. It's a dream job, something I'd given up any hope of ever achieving. And then it's handed to me, at the worst possible time."

"Do you see yourself in that job? I can't imagine not being a chef."

"I guess I've seen myself in that job for so long,

I'd stopped thinking it could be anything more than a dream. If I took it, I would earn so much more money. I might even be able to buy a house. Put money away in savings. Finally be an adult like the kind in normal Life and not the Crisis Edition."

He cuts into his pancakes and takes a bite, chewing for a very long time. "It's a nice city," he finally says. "You'd like it there, I think. I'd miss you, obviously, but I think you'd like it."

This is so hard. It's like I'm being pulled in two different directions. My brain says go, but my heart says stay.

"But I don't have to go to Santa Fe! I'm really liking Mae'd..."

That's a half-truth. In actuality, I'm still really stressed about it, and I'm beginning to think I don't have what it takes to run a real business. But I don't want to leave if Austin and I are just starting to pursue a thing and he's going to have his own restaurant. "Maybe I could be a hostess at your place?" I say, hopefully.

"Uh, actually. I was going to say I think you should take the job in Santa Fe. These kinds of opportunities don't just come up."

"But what about...." I don't want to be too presumptuous. "Our garden."

"I can look after our garden, believe it or not, on

my own." He knows what I really meant, though. It's written all over his face in bold letters. "Our...friendship will survive across miles."

Friendship? Was that a euphemism? Was that a hint that he doesn't want to deal with all the risks after all? We finish our breakfast in silence, and by the time I get the courage to ask, he stands and moves to the counter to place his dish in the sink. "I have to run to the garden center and pick up some fertilizer. It's supposed to drizzle later, so I want to get that down and transplant all the starters first."

"Okay," I say instead of all the questions swirling in my head.

And when he leaves, I'm left wondering what just happened.

And then Logan calls.

"Hey," he says. "I saw something that reminded me of you."

"Really, what was it?"

"We went on this tour and saw the Palace of the Governors. The guy said it was built in 1610 and is the oldest building in the United States. Your cute history facts popped in my mind, and it just seemed like something you'd enjoy."

"I totally would've loved to have seen that."

"It was cool. I bought you something there that I think you'll like."

He tells me Native Americans were selling their wares, and he found a pottery vendor that had amazing vases. It's sort of swoony how he's thinking about me. Especially when he says, "Just because you're dating other people doesn't mean I'm not going to try to woo you too."

Unf.

Then he adds, "Have you given your answer to Santa Fe yet?"

"I said I'd tell them Monday."

"Please say no. Even if you decide you don't want me as your boyfriend, I don't think I could stand not having you in my life."

Whoa. That was real clear. Clearer than the conversation with Austin.

"Logan, get your ass off the phone and help me carry the equipment," someone shouts.

"I gotta run," he says. "I'll call you back later."

When I'm off the phone, I sit at the table and think.

And think.

About Austin. About Logan.

I don't need to wait until the end of the tour. I already know who I'm choosing.

Me.

SUMMER LOVIN

EPISODE 6

My dating season has come to a close, and I'm ready for a Hot Boyfriend Summer...

Almost every single thing in my life has changed over the past year.

New job.

New me.

New knowledge.

Ah, to be young again, with the wisdom I have gained over a year's worth of dating-as-a-competitive-sport.

If only I'd had just about an inch more before I made my commitment…

ONE

"Under certain circumstances, profanity provides a relief denied even to prayer."
—Mark Twain

WHEN A GROUP of shouting people pop out of nowhere, it startles a person.

Historians say early usages of the word *fuck* actually meant "to strike" rather than the act of sexual relations. *Strike* is what I do when "To Mae'd!" blares at me from many unexpected mouths as I enter the kitchen.

The crowd gathered around the island receives a

barrage of expletives from me in response to their unexpected presence. "Holyfuckityfuckingfuckerfuck," I screech, swinging my Passion Party bag and rocketing at least five feet off the floor.

"Oomph," barrels out of a leather-vested mountain of a man when my sneaker-clad foot connects with his groin.

Gasps fill the room, silencing the thundering pulse in my ears, as my newly purchased dildo flies across the room and knocks over a tripod holding a phone.

Hearty laughter drifts up from the fallen device and a voice that sounds a lot like Will's asks, "Did a flying dick just knock me over? Is this payback for seeing mine?"

What is going on? It takes a split second to regain my senses and realize I'm in the midst of friends rather than nefarious foes. Everyone assembled displays various stages of disbelief.

Charlotte, wide-eyed, fumbling to reassemble the tripod.

Ryan, slow-blinking like he's recently consumed a mountain of gummies.

Dune and a few of his biker friends, mouths open and brows raised.

Ruth, Ryan's mom, paused mid-fold of a kitchen towel.

Prez hunched over.

Oh *dear*. I kicked the president of a motorcycle gang in the balls. In my defense, what's he doing in my kitchen on a Friday evening?

"Are you okay?" Ruth sashays over to him with concern on her face.

"Yeah," he grunts. "She's got a firm foot."

Thankfully Prez truly has balls of steel, because within a minute he rises from his curled over position with a semi-grin on his face.

"I'm good."

"I'm so sorry," I say. "I wasn't expecting anyone to be here."

With the smirkiest of smirks, Ryan glances at the rod laying on the counter. "Apparently not."

Everyone's eyes dart to the eight-inch elephant in the room.

"I, uh, that's not for me..." I say to the raised eyebrows around the room. "I had an idea for a side project... Laid With Love. Get it?"

That's the truth. Obviously, it's in the beginning stages, but five days ago, after Austin urged me to move to Santa Fe and Logan asked me to stay, I met up with Charlotte and made the most adult decision of my life.

I'm choosing myself.

A guy to accompany me on the journey is just extra frosting on the Mae'd With Love cake.

Charlotte snatches up the rogue toy and pockets it. "I love your idea. That's brilliant." She crosses over to me, wearing an adorable Mae'd With Love T-shirt.

"I'll buy one," says Angel. "There's nothing wrong with a little self-love while your man is away on a road trip with his brothers."

"That's hot, babe," Jackal says. He looks over at me. "How much do you want for it? I'll buy it right now."

"Oh, um, it's not for sale yet. I'm still in the developmental phase." I tilt my head at Charlotte. "What's going on?"

"It's a Kickstarter Kickoff party for Mae'd With Love."

It's my turn to be shocked. "What? Really?"

"Yes! I sent e-vites to everyone to surprise you."

She takes my hand and leads me over to a laptop surrounded by balloons on the breakfast table. "See? I've got the account all set up for you. We're going to raise lots of money." She dips her head forward and whispers, "Because mama needs to rent some space and buy her own kiln so she can quit It's Clay Time. Just like we discussed."

"Wow, you work so fast. You remain goals." We had

discussed it. Endlessly, even. During our talk, she suggested crowdfunding, where I'll receive online donations to help fund my business, and frankly, though I hate to admit it, Charlotte really never is wrong. I just sort of assumed I'd have time to dilly-dally.

"I didn't want you to lose momentum"—she waves her arm to the room—"and neither do they."

I hug every single person with my eyes. "Thank you all so much."

"We got your back," Dune says.

My heart swells in my chest that these people are here to support me. Although. I can't help but notice that Austin is noticeably absent.

"Of course, if I'd known you would literally kick people," Charlotte says, "I would have suggested everyone gently yell."

"At least she didn't poison him," Logan teases from the tripod.

I walk closer to see his smiling face surrounded by his band members.

"Hi," I say. "Thanks for being here."

"Sorry I can't be there in person." He flashes white teeth at me. "You really know how to make an entrance."

"I'll say," Prez grumbles.

"That was kind of cool," Dune says with an

amused grin. "You looked like you were in the Matrix."

I apologize again to Prez. "Must be the yoga."

He throws his heavy arm over my shoulder and gives me a squeeze. "Let's never talk about it again. Yeah?"

"Yeah." I smile and glance at the champagne bottle nestled in a bucket of ice and the bouquet of red roses on the counter. My people all wearing Mae'd With Love T-shirts. I feel like everything's going my way, which is a new feeling. Brand new. Still in the packaging, even. I could really get used to it.

There's no time to inquire about Austin's whereabouts, because the party people want to party.

"I can't believe you did this," I say to Charlotte.

"I can't believe you cursed like that. And speaking of fucks..." She laughs and removes the elephant from her pocket. "It is so genius to expand."

I take it from her. "I don't do well with surprises."

"Must be the feeling of lack of control."

"Maybe? I just like to be prepared to have fun."

"Then gird your loins," a twangy voice says.

The people smiling part like the Red Sea, revealing what must be a mirage walking toward me in a Mae'd With Love T-shirt. This time, my scream isn't from fear.

"Granny Mae! What... How...?"

Her cornflower blue eyes twinkle with merriment. "Close your mouth before you catch flies and get over here."

In two seconds, I'm wrapped in her thin arms, ample bosom pressed to my heart while she explains that Austin made arrangements to fly her out at the last minute for my party.

"He said it wouldn't be right for the namesake not to be here. And I have to agree."

"Me too." I smile at Austin, who is hanging back, hands in jeans pockets. "How long are you staying?"

"Only until Sunday. What's that in your hand?"

"This?" I look down at it in hopes it will disappear. "It's a...massage tool."

I'm not ready to tell her about my new plan for the business. She's not a prude by any stretch of the imagination, but I founded Mae'd on her likeness and...oh no, what if she nixes the idea?

"Ah, for a minute there, I thought it was one of those vibratory things. Maybe I'll use it later. My back is a little stiff from the flight."

"I love her *so much*," I hear Charlotte say.

Austin intervenes and crosses over to us with quick strides. "I'll put that away for you and take Miss Mae's suitcase to your room."

While he's gone, I introduce everyone to Granny

Mae, and she doesn't even flinch at the ratio of leather vests in the room because she's cool like that.

When Austin returns, Ryan asks in front of everyone about the Santa Fe job.

"It turns out that when I really thought about what sparks joy, it was with what I have now, not the dream I had in college," I say. "I have grown as a person. And not just because of all the pasta I get now."

Over his shoulder, Austin's gaze meets mine, but his face is unreadable.

"Thank you so much for getting me the opportunity, though." I look around at the cute Mae'd shirts everyone is wearing, and the box of more, waiting to become backer rewards. "And for making the T-shirts."

"I think you've folded enough of his that you earned them," Ruth says.

We laugh, but really I have, and Logan tells everyone goodbye because he has to go onstage. "Congrats, Chloe. So proud of you," he says in his sign off. "I'll call you later. Enjoy your party."

I give him a little wave, feeling Austin's stare bore through my head.

"So, what exactly *are* your plans for Mae'd?" Dune asks. "Because we need to talk about incorporating. We should probably make a list."

"Well, let's hit publish on this Kickstarter first, and then we'll talk."

Charlotte beams. "Let's do it."

Holding Granny Mae's hand, I press publish.

They clap, and I *woo*, and Austin uncorks the champagne, spewing foam down from the chilled bottle.

"To the next phase of Mae'd," Charlotte says.

Our glasses clink, and the celebration continues with Granny Mae herself charming everyone with tales of how she came up with certain recipes.

They love her. I love her.

Austin remains on the periphery, whipping up hors d'oeuvres, glancing up to smile occasionally. As the night goes on, we break into clusters of conversations, the way it happens once people get some champagne and snacks to break the ice.

"Tell me more about this new idea," Charlotte urges when we're alone in a corner of the kitchen.

She listens as I explain how Anna at It's Clay Time had invited me to her Passion Party. Sitting in a circle of women passing flavored lube around, I then recalled Mildred's frequent restocks and the wide world that romance novels had opened to me.

What happened next was nothing short of a miracle.

While holding a set of anal beads, fingering them

like a rosary, thinking I needed to get laid, the idea came to me like a vision straight from the heavens.

"Only you could think of something so clever while being so sacrilegious." She sips her sparkling water. "I'm impressed."

"Life is never a straight path, so why should I try to follow one? If I learned anything this last year, it's that I'm nuanced—good girl and bad girl—and my business can reflect that side of me."

She clinks her glass to mine. "Amen. Now, go put Austin out of his misery, will you?"

I look over to where he stands, listening intently to something Granny Mae is telling him as he refills a serving dish with freshly fried tortilla chips and homemade guac.

"Yeah, it's time."

Charlotte beckons Granny Mae over to explain how she makes her onion dip, and I snag a red rose from the vase.

"Hey, you," Austin says when I approach.

"Can we porch?" I ask.

He nods and follows me outside, where we both try and fail to start the conversation while awkwardly speaking over each other.

"I already know wh—"
"I wanted to—"
"No, it's—"

"No, you—"

"Fine—"

"I hav—"

"I unders—"

Any MC heroine in a situation like this has but two choices: slap the hero across the face, or kiss him.

I opt for the second, just a soft peck, enough to shut him up, but enough to light me up like the moon hanging in the sky.

"First... I can't thank you enough for getting Granny Mae here. Best surprise ever."

"It wasn't easy keeping it a secret. But she had to be here. She's the foundation of your business. And your life. Wish I could've been here to see your entrance. I heard all about it from Ryan. He said you cursed up a storm."

"Technically, there was no storm. I merely struck. Verbally. Did you know your brain doesn't consider swear words as words? They're just blobs of emotion stored in a different part of your brain than all the other words we know."

"I didn't know that." He looks at me like I look at art—full of wonder and appreciation. "I'm glad you're staying here in Colorado."

"Glad you mentioned that." I look down at the flower in my hands. "When I told people about the job, you were the only one who didn't try to influence my decision by how it would make *them* feel."

He tilts my chip up to meet his dark gaze. "I'm sorry. I should have been more honest about my feelings. Of course I wanted you to—"

"No, you respected *my* feelings. And that's why... Austin, will you accept my rose?"

TWO

IF LIFE WERE PERFECT, Austin would reach out with misty eyes, take my rose, and utter something romantic, maybe poetically comparing me to the delicate flower I'm offering him, and we'd live happily ever after in our house on the hill.

Unfortunately, it's still an imperfect real world.

"Chloe," Granny Mae interrupts, bursting out the door and preventing Austin from answering me. "Dune is taking me for a ride on his motorcycle. I'll be back soon."

My head whips to her petite frame. "What?"

Dune steps outside. "She'll be fine. I'll be right back, Mae. I had to park my bike down the street to keep everything a surprise."

He hustles past us with long, booted strides, and

I leave Austin to follow my wayward granny across the porch and down the steps onto the driveway.

"Well, wait." I finally stop her at the curb. "I don't know about this."

"I do," she says. "I'm going to take some pictures to post on my FriendsOfFriends account. Spice things up a bit. If you want to catch big fish, you need the right bait."

Though her dating phase unsettles me, I say, "Oh, I can drive you. I have seat belts."

She pats my arm like she's reassuring a small child. "Don't be silly, Chloe. I've never been on a motorcycle, so I'm going to cross it off my bucket list. The women at Bingo will be so envious. Did I tell you my neighbor created an account on the site? She's been snatching up all my rejects. She'll be hard-pressed to come up with a biker."

I peek over my shoulder at Austin for help, but he's grinning like he thinks this is the best idea in all the land. I disagree. It's not that I think she's too fragile to ride on a motorcycle... Okay, maybe it is.

"Wait for us," Ruth calls out. "Prez is going to take me for a ride, too."

If I'm not mistaken, she has an extra swing in her hips as she saunters down the driveway with Dune's father hot on her leather loafers. There's no mistaking the look he gives her or the way she twinkles like the stars when he leaves us to retrieve his Harley.

"I'm so glad you came into Ryan's life," she confides. "If not, I wouldn't be here and I wouldn't have met Prez. Thank you for staying friends with my son after he broke up with you."

"You're welcome," I say, not interested in correcting her about Ryan's and my breakup, because the thunderous roar of Dune's bike rumbles down the road and pulls onto the blacktop.

"Put this on," he tells Granny, offering a helmet.

As she slips the black helmet over her silvery blonde bob, the glee on her face erases twenty years, but not my hesitation.

Austin appears beside me and drapes an arm over my shoulders. "I'm sure I don't have to say it," he directs at Dune.

"Nope," he replies.

"You get me?"

"Yep."

Side note: Dune and Austin's conversation dynamics are so fascinating to me. Somehow, they've found a way to communicate with as few words as possible. And it works.

"You sure?"

"Yeah, man. I'll treat her like my own."

And that's enough reassurance for me to give my

blessing. "Have fun, and remember camera angles are important."

"How do I get on this thing?" Granny asks.

Austin helps her on the back of the bike and once Ruth settles behind Prez, she waves as they roar away at what I can only consider a snail's pace for Dune.

"Well, I guess a party is not a party unless your grandmother rides off on the back of a motorcycle," I muse on our way back to the house.

"A party is not a party until the guest of honor receives her gift."

"My gift?" I stop in the same spot we were in before Grannies Gone Wild happened. "This isn't a gift party. I can't accept a gift." I shake my head. "You've done too much for me."

He places a finger on my lips to halt my words, and leans down to whisper in my ear, "I need to see you in my bedroom for a moment."

Well, then. I take back everything I just said.

He opens the door for me, and the party's still going strong in the backyard. Laughter and music filter into the living room from the open patio door, so I feel less guilty about leaving the guests to detour and sneak into Austin's room.

"You didn't have to get me anything. Granny Mae is the best gift ever."

"You might change your mind when I give you this."

The lock booms like a cannon as it clicks into place. He rests his back against the wood and gives a chin nod to the flower still in my grasp. "What were you saying about your rose before we were interrupted? Did you forget about what you asked me?"

The air seizes in my lungs. "It's not that I forgot, but it kind of seemed like the universe sent a signal that maybe the timing isn't right."

He pushes off the wall and moves closer. "Ask me again."

Every step he takes closer increases my heartbeat until it's banging against my chest. "Will you accept my rose?"

"Did you really think I wouldn't?"

He takes it from me and then his lips are on mine and my hands are in his hair, free to roam and explore without fear or guilt binding them.

Our moans mingle, and it's like kissing him for the first time. Every swipe of his tongue against mine creates a new sensation I've never experienced.

It's like discovering what it's like to be with him all over again. The growling sound from his throat, the caress from his fingertips against my breast, the ache in my chest that seems more poignant.

He walks me back toward the bed and breaks away when the back of my knees hit the mattress.

"I'm going to give you your gift."

"Oh. Now?"

He nods and wets his lips. "I think you'll want this gift. Are you ready for it?"

"Really, it's okay. You don't have to," I say greedily, wanting to continue the make-out session with him. "We don't know how long they'll be gone, so let me kiss you senseless a little longer?"

He reaches between my legs and palms the epicenter of my lust, rubbing the heel of his hand against the electrified bundle of nerves.

I'm sure I'll love his present, but his magical hand has me under a spell. I don't want to seem ungrateful, so I shove my selfish desires away. "I'm ready and then I'll kiss you senseless with gratitude?"

His teeth scrape against the shell of my ear while he continues to work my body into a frenzy. "My gift is to kiss your pussy senseless."

My thighs clench at his dirty talking. This moment seems surreal. Like it's too good to be true, and the universe is messing with me and I'll wake up in the morning to realize it's been a dream.

"Climb on the bed." His bossy tone leaves no room for disagreement.

Not that I was going to, mind you. It would take

an army of clowns to stop my lunge onto the soft-as-a-cloud mattress.

"You can't make a sound," he says, removing the bottom half of my clothes with skillful hands.

He trails the rose along my skin, from foot to thigh, caressing it over my panties before he leans down to remove them with his teeth. It's a perfect combination of romance and caveman. Heaven help me.

"Fuck," he murmurs, staring at my most private part. "Lie back so I can taste you."

My pulse races as I follow instructions, granting him access to feast upon me.

"Did you know rose petals are edible?"

"I knew this," I whisper.

His dark eyes flit to mine with a devilish glint in them. He plucks a petal and drops it on my bare pussy. "I deserve her"—he plucks another—"I deserve her not…"

He continues on until the last petal remains and I reach in and stop him from removing it, because it's not true. "You deserve me. Trust me."

With a groan, he dives between my legs, like I'm an altar for him to worship from. My heart thrashes as he teases me, lifting each rose petal with a sensual tongue flick and eating them until there is nothing left between us.

"God, I can't wait for you to come on my face."

He hooks my leg over his shoulder, and I quiver with anticipation as he plants lingering kisses and quick nips along the sensitive area of my inner thighs, working his way to the sweet spot that's already dripping for him. It's like he's circling prey, building the excitement before moving in for the kill. His tongue drags along my seam and I fist the comforter in my hands, arching my back.

"You're so wet," he says, sucking my lucky lips into his mouth.

"I'm so turned on, I may come before you get started," I pant out.

He moans, and then finally ends the torture. My whole body exhales as he sucks, nibbles, blows, and licks with a voracity that increases the warm feeling low in my belly to an inferno. I bite down on my lip to keep from crying out, and prop on my elbows to watch him—to memorize this moment. He looks up at me with hooded eyes drunk with desire, and ah, God, inserts a finger. It's too much.

Too good.

There is no time to warn him I'm coming; my body shatters into a million blissful pieces.

He gathers them all and breaks me again when he groans and slides in another finger, rolling my orgasm into another.

"Wow," I whisper when my body calms.

He moves up, eyes never leaving mine, and I wrap my legs around his hips, grinding against the swell in his jeans.

"I want to give back," I say.

The way he bites his lip and the strain on his face tells me he wants it too.

"Not now. I want to wait until the third date."

As disappointed as I am, I respect his decision. It's super hot fooling around like this, but there's a party going on.

He kisses the disappointment away, and we ready ourselves to rejoin the guests.

"How did Logan take it?" he asks on our way to the door.

"I haven't told him yet."

He tilts his head, hand on the doorknob. "Why not?"

"Because I feel the right way to do it is face-to-face."

His brow furrows. "So you're still dating both of us."

"No! I'm only dating you! He just doesn't know that part yet."

"You just described dating two people."

"It's more a case of timelines not matching up?"

"You don't understand timelines, do you?"

I sigh. "It's tempting to avoid the conversation in person because it makes me uncomfortable, but I think he deserves more than a phone call. The internet experts say it's best to break up in person and I agree."

"The internet experts?"

"Yes. It's respectful and kind."

He nods. "Okay."

I don't believe his okay.

"Is that the male version of 'it's fine' when it's not really fine?"

"No. I get it." He drops a kiss to my forehead and swats me on the butt. See? Romance and caveman.

"Do you? I could easily text or call him, ghost him, but I don't know, talking to him in-person seems like the right thing to do. The adult thing."

He doesn't seem to understand how monumental this decision is, blowing it off as though we're still in the place we were a few days ago, but I know the difference. I'm all in. And I show it by kissing away the frown on his face before returning to our guests.

THREE

IT'S weird to dodge a sexcapade with Logan right after pruning the nether region specifically for the guy in the next room. But that's exactly what I'm doing as I dress for an outing with Granny and Charlotte. I've no right to complain about feelings of discomfort regarding Logan's amorous advances, because if I insist on doing the right thing, then I have to take my lumps.

"So, is it bad to ask if Laid With Love is coming soon?"

I laugh off Logan's loaded question, but my attempt to seem casual sounds a little too high-pitched and nervous to my ears. "Well, I still have lots of details to work out, like what recipe I'll include with the products to keep it on brand." Even though I know he wasn't really going for an actual business summary with his question, I continue on, hoping to distract him from his horniness. "I also need to finalize the design, and figure out packaging. Ryan can help with the design. I'm thinking I want something sleek and minimal. Black and pink with a tiny heart dotting the i. Hm. What else? Do I want a new logo to separate the two divisions or the same with different colors? So many decisions. So summing up, yes, it's bad to ask."

None of my ramble succeeded in distracting him from his aim, which is to orgasm. "Well, as you know, I'm a very bad boy."

Normally, I'd ask how bad, encourage him to fill my ears with filthy talk, but times have changed. He doesn't know times have changed, so now it's just awkward when I don't press him to elaborate on his claim of naughtiness.

Instead of hopping onto the bed and sliding down my panties, I have to roll my lips inward to stop myself from ending things right here and now. I know Austin thinks I should just do it on the phone and get it done, but that's the coward's way out of the relationship.

Perhaps I should at least give him a hint about what's coming? No pun intended. The articles I read about breaking up with a person you actually like said not to do the "we need to talk" thing because there's nothing worse than the dread that follows hearing that phrase from someone you care about. As much as I want to not string him along, I agree with their advice because I've been in that position. When someone says that to you, it's obvious what follows.

"How's Arizona?" I ask to navigate away from this landscape painted with sexual undertones to a shade more neutral.

"It's so damn hot." His voice lowers into a raspy hush. "The kind of heat that makes you feel as if your body will catch fire if you don't get some relief. You know what I mean? You're almost ready to beg for some wetness to extinguish the burn in your body."

"I'm not a big fan of that kind of climate. My temperature limit is probably eighty-five degrees with no humidity." I shimmy into jeans and a vintage Rolling Stones tee as he continues to make the arid weather sound like a lover tormenting him. And if he could only get some relief, he'll survive another day. Usually I'd say something risqué like how can I relieve that for you, tell him to stroke his cock, use all my sexy romance novel tricks, but that can't happen anymore.

"Did you know petrified wood is their official state fossil?"

As I slip on red flats, I want to kick myself with them for my choice of words.

"Wood, huh? So the semi in my pants could halfway qualify."

There's really no good segue into another topic but I try anyway. "Speaking of wood...would you believe I have to go?"

"Really?" Swear he moans a little. "That's a shame, because I'd love to come."

Man, he's *good*. Gotta give props to his ability to sway the conversation back to phone sex. If he ever quits the music industry, this might be a lucrative gig for him.

"I'm sorry. Charlotte arranged for us to look at a few commercial spaces today for my shop with Granny Mae before she leaves tomorrow."

He takes it in stride and after I assure him I don't have time to finger myself, we hang up. Ugh. How will I continue to sidestep his phone-sex advances until he returns? And not to brag, but I know there will be more because...

That's all we do on the phone? My brain backtracks through our conversations since he's been away and the ratio of dirty talk ones versus just regular chit-chatting is alarming.

On my way to the kitchen, I realize something else important. Even if there were no Austin, and I didn't plan on breaking up with him, I'd almost be perturbed there were no questions of value about my new endeavor. Of course, how can I be bothered by the shaky construction of our relationship when I helped build the lewd foundation on which it rests?

Oh, well. Doesn't matter. In a few weeks, when he returns, it's all going to come crashing down.

"YOU HAVE to come back for my baby shower, Miss Mae," Charlotte pleads with her. "I won't take no for an answer."

"I wouldn't miss it, sugar. If I have a date with a new beau, I'll cancel it."

We are simultaneously planning the baby shower while looking at rental spaces for Mae'd, and I am triple-tasking trying to muster up the courage to tell my grandmother about my new plans for the business.

"I've already set up the Pinterest board for the baby shower," I inform Charlotte as we wander around a warehouse style space that is affordable, yet spacious.

"It's a little early, don't you think?" Charlotte balks.

"No. I found the perfect theme."

"She kept me up half the night talking about that site and showing me pictures of cookies," Granny says, walking over to inspect the counter running along the back wall.

And she kept *me* up the other half snoring, but I don't even care because she's here with us.

"What's the theme?" Charlotte asks, checking out a sunlit nook in the far corner with a glass curio case.

"Baby Is Coming. That's it. That's the theme. You love Game of Thrones—well, the good seasons—and look at this..."

I whip out my phone and show her the adorable cookies custom-shaped like onesies and decorated with deer, lion, wolf, and dragon insignias, as well as precious rectangular ones with Baby Is Coming written on them.

"Oh my God. I love it," she says, giving her full approval on everything I pinned. "Okay, that's settled. Now, what about this space? This area would be perfect for the Laid With Love line, don't you think?"

I wave off her words, trying to signal her to zip it, but it's too late.

"What's Laid With Love?" Granny Mae asks.

Charlotte cringes. "You didn't tell her?"

"Tell me what?"

"Oh, nothing. Chloe wanted—"

She realizes her mistake and tries to correct it,

but it's not her fault I haven't told sweet Granny Mae about my dirty idea yet, so instead of hiding the truth, I cut her off. "I want to expand the business with something I can make quickly, with less of the painstaking painting details."

"Well, that sounds like a smart idea. What kind of things? She said Laid With Love. Is that some sort of bedding?"

"No."

She rests her elbows on the counter, chin in hand. "Is this some kind of guessing game? I could guess all day, or you could just tell me?"

Charlotte bites back a laugh, and I blurt it out. "It's sex toys." Granny slowly blinks, but lets me continue. "A coworker of mine started a side business selling them and I went to support her, and while I was there, I was thinking about Mildred's order for the bookstore, and thought this would be a perfect add-on to sell. Plus...making the items for Mae'd is time-consuming, so with this additional income, maybe I can get ahead. But your name is attached, so...if you feel weird or reluctant, I don't have to do it."

She leans up from the counter. "Why would I feel weird? I think it's a fantastic idea. I'm so proud of you, Chloe, and everything you're accomplishing." Her voice breaks a bit. "You're a successful businesswoman. The ladies at Bingo are going to shit and fall back in it when I tell them about this."

I cross to her for a hug. Gah. Everything is falling into place for me.

"Phew," Charlotte says. "I was going to feel horrible if it didn't have a happy ending. Now that we don't have to hide Laid With Love, what do you think about this space?"

"There's a drain in the floor and those back stairs are really steep," I say, picking apart the wide area. "I couldn't let the baby crawl around in here. Should we have a mimosa bar?"

"Chloe, there will be a *kiln* in there," Charlotte says. "Why on earth would the baby be crawling around recklessly? The drain is the least of your problems. Definitely yes, on mimosas."

"All babies are reckless," Granny Mae adds, ominously. "Chloe was dragging herself across the floor with one arm before she could crawl."

"Good thing I've trained with you," Charlotte mutters. "Add that to the baby rules—no crawling before Mama is ready."

"Don't worry about training," Granny Mae clucks like a mother hen. "You can plan everything perfectly, but babies make their own rules."

"I think following the rules are more for me to feel like I'm doing things right," Charlotte says, absently rubbing her barely there baby bump. "It's scary thinking of all the sacrifices. I'm going to live in a fortress of baby gates."

"Don't fret." Granny rubs her back. "Your instincts will kick in when the baby is in your arms. Don't underestimate the effect of love. People seem to forget that's what binds us together. We make sacrifices for those we care about. Take Austin..." She points at me. "Overheard him apologizing for missing a meeting with some finance person because he picked me up at the airport. Heard him say he was doing something for a very important person."

Ah, why is he so good to me? Truly, it's me that doesn't deserve him.

"Speaking of Austin," she continues, "what are you doing about those boys?"

Since she opened the can of worms, I fuss to them for a bit about whether I'm truly doing the right thing with Logan or being a righteous coward. "He deserves face-to-face, I'm sure, but what do I do in the meantime? It feels like I'm stringing him along. Past Chloe would have stopped taking his calls all together until he came back to town. I feel simultaneously guilty and extremely mature about this whole breakup. It's a strange place to be in."

"My dearest friend"—Charlotte places a hand on my arm—"the entirety of your mind seems like a strange place to be in. But listen. I need this done and settled for my own inner peace. You're giving me Braxton-Hicks."

"You're still in your first trimester."

"What do you know about pregnancy?"

"I must admit, not much."

"I've got a book about every phase of pregnancy you can read once you have the time to focus on me again. And I need your focus on me. So, here's what you're going to do. I have miles from honeymooning, and they'll get you to Arizona to break up with Logan, to his face, and back again before dinner."

"That's a superb idea," Granny Mae says. "We can go to the airport together tomorrow, and you can move on with your life."

"I am not taking your miles!" Am I? It would make things easier and end the charade with Logan so he doesn't get hurt.

"Yes, you goddamn are. Or else I'll...I'll...I'll make everyone play baby shower games."

"I'll book a flight."

Welp. That's settled.

FOUR

"I HATE FLYING MORE than I hate passwords with a capital letter, number, and a punctuation mark," Roger grumbles on our Uber ride to the airport.

As promised, I booked a flight to Arizona to dump Logan, and since Austin had to meet up with his boss, and doesn't know what I'm planning, who better to take us there than the best Uber driver in the world?

"I'm not a fan either," I admit. "Maybe you can just drive me there?"

"Don't be silly, Chloe." Granny Mae pats my leg. "The cost would be outrageous. And even if it weren't, you'll be fine."

"She's right. You'll be okay," Roger says. "I'm not afraid of anything bad happening to me. I just hate being shoved up next to people and fighting for the armrest."

I look out the window at the tall trees and sweet earth that will soon be out of sight. "I loathe that too. Right now, calling him seems like the better option. I think I'll just call him. Kindness is overrated."

"Listen to me," Granny Mae says with no mercy. "When did you become such a scaredy cat? This is not the girl who picked up everything and moved to another state to follow a dream. Or the one who started her own business. And now a side business. You've got more businesses than I've got bras."

"Easy for you to say. There was a lot of turbulence on that flight. And you hate bras!"

She arches a stern brow at me.

"Okay, okay," I relent. "Maybe I just need to practice so I don't end up babbling or getting tongue-tied. I do that a lot."

"You've always done that since you could talk." She pulls a Chapstick out of her bag and runs it over her lips. "Do what you need to do, but you're doing this. Roger, you're Logan."

"Yes, ma'am," he says.

The experts agree it's important to get straight to the point and not drag it out, so I rip the Band-Aid off. "Hi, Logan. I'm breaking up with you. It's over, and I wish you the best in life. You're amazing. Bye."

Granny Mae's chin melds with her neck. "What kind of breakup is that? If that's the case, then yes, you need to call him. You need to say your piece but realize it's going to be uncomfortable for him. I've had some experience with this lately. Here, let me show you how it's done."

Roger's amused eyes meet mine in the rear-view mirror.

"Logan, honey, as much as I've enjoyed our time together, and I have...that night after Bingo"—she fans herself—"whew... but things aren't meant to be between us. You're amazing in the sack—"

"Granny *Mae*," I screech with owl eyes.

"Well, you have to stroke their egos, Chloe."

Roger chuckles. "Just be honest with him about why you're breaking up. You don't have to plan it word for word. It's simple. Treat him how you'd want to be treated and remember he's got feelings too. I'm sure he had an inkling you'd end up with the other guy. I certainly did."

"This sucks," I say. "It's hard enough breaking up with someone you don't like, much less someone you actually enjoyed spending time with."

But I won't back out. I remind myself of that as we get closer to our destination. Roger and Granny Mae fill the rest of the car ride chatting with each other and I push away thoughts of what I'm going to do in a few hours and focus on enjoying the last of my time with Granny Mae.

Much too soon, Roger is dropping us off in front of the airport. He hops out to open Granny Mae's door and I grab her plaid duffel bag.

"You come see me, if you're ever in North Carolina," she tells him. "I've got plenty of room around my table for more friends."

"Will do," he says. And he looks like he truly might follow her there.

Since I may never see his smiling face again, I hug him.

"Thank you," I say. "I truly appreciate you and I'm so glad my app picked you that night."

"You're my favorite customer," he says. "Don't forget to rate me."

"As if I would ever forget."

Once Granny Mae is safely checked in, and I've hugged her a million times, she says, "Obviously, I have my favorite between your two men, but whoever you end up with is lucky to have you. Never forget your worth."

"I'm lucky to have you," I say and kiss her cheek. "I don't want to leave you."

"Now you're just trying to miss your flight," she says with a smile.

Possibly. Ha. I kid. I kid.

After one last hug, I set off for my own flight. As I board, I think of all the things I'm going to say to Logan. When the plane picks up speed and leaves the ground, I close my eyes and picture that house on the hill. It's Austin I see with me, so I feel confident I'm doing the right thing.

I'M like my very own "How it started... How it's going" meme.

How it started:

1. I planned and waited for the right moment *after* Logan's set so as not to upset him *before* he went on stage. No one wants an upset drummer, thrashing their sticks out of rhythm. Least of all me.
2. I expressed my reason for ending things honestly and with compassion for his feelings.
3. I didn't just spring it on him and then bolt out of the venue.

How it's going:

Those blasted internet experts said to prepare for different reactions. Of course, it's impossible to know how Logan would react to the news of our breakup. I prepared myself for surprise, anger, or possibly sadness. He gave me the one thing I never expected—refusal.

"I, uh, know this must be shocking, but you can't really say no."

"I don't want to break up," he repeats, placing a hand on the wall above my head, looking down at me with confusion. "And I don't think you realize I'm the right guy for you. But I am."

Is this a thing, like refusing to accept a divorce? I'm ill-prepared for his reaction. Once upon a different time, I probably would've held back the truth, but not now.

"Look, full disclosure," I say, gently. "I've always been in love with Austin, and I want to give things a real shot with him."

He rakes his teeth over the corner of his lip, studying me like I'm a puzzle to solve. "Do you? Or is it just easy and comfortable to be with the guy you already live with, rather than try to make it work with someone who's on the road a lot?"

This is not going well. It pains me to say it, but I do...

"Logan, *you* are what's easy and comfortable."

He shakes his head, slowly. "No, I'm not. He's your security blanket, Chloe. And you've wrapped yourself up in him. You don't even realize it, so I can't be mad at you. He is a safety net and I'm the scary unknown."

Tears prick my eyelids. I was so worried about sparing him any pain; I didn't consider how it would feel for me to do this. It hurts to hurt him, if I'm being honest. I blink back the tears welling in my eyes. He does not know the unknowns are far more terrifying with Austin than the unknowns with him. But something tells me he's not going to give an inch on this and maybe it's the kinder thing to do to let him think he's right.

I want to reach out and comfort him but I slide my hands in my pockets so I don't. "I just need to see where this goes. I'm sorry. I really am. I don't want to hurt you…"

He looks at a spot on the wall above my head before finally meeting my gaze again. "I have another show in ten minutes, Chlo." Oh. Oops. "How am I supposed to react to this?"

Face-to-face breakups are horrible. No wonder people go the childish route and do it over the phone. I'd rather have the innocence of a child any day over this. Not one article emphasized the worst part of doing it this way—seeing their *face*.

"Put it in your music?" Hopefully he'll be kind too. On second thought, I shouldn't have suggested that if I don't want to be blasted on the radio someday. I give him another option. "Or go for a run later? Let out your stress on the pavement?"

"Is there a ring on your finger?" he asks instead.

"No." Weird question, but who am I to judge his process of accepting things ending.

He gives me a curt nod and steps away. "I've got to get on stage."

And with that, he turns and stalks away, pushing the door open with enough force to knock it against the wall. He continues down the bright hallway without looking back. And then he's gone.

Well. Guess that's over.

I blow out a breath and stand in the silence for a while, staring at the closed door. That saying about opening and closing doors filters through my mind. God, I hope I never have to open another door, because closing them is fucking hard. This is by no means what I'd consider a success, but hopefully, if I'm lucky, he won't hate me. I don't want him to hate me. What did I expect? That he'd smile and say okay, let's be friends? My relationship with him wasn't the same as Dune and Ryan, which is probably why I was able to remain friends with them. Part of me feels terrible, but the other part of me feels like I have removed a crushing weight from my shoulders.

On the flight home, as I soar above the clouds, staring out the window, all the pent-up emotions that have been held back burst free like a river through a dam.

Austin and I have no obstacles.

Finally, there's nothing between us.

A giddy feeling replaces the mopiness. When Roger picks me back up at the airport, having apparently expected me to survive both flights, he tells me I'm amazing and mature for completing my mission. I'm feeling less guilty with every mile that ticks away on the odometer, and by the time he pulls in the driveway, I'm downright excited to tell Austin.

"You're the best," I tell Roger before he drives away. "Thank you again."

Austin's truck isn't here, so I rush inside and do something to spoil *him* for a change.

By the time he walks in the kitchen, I've prepared gourmet sandwiches, just like he taught me, complete with tomatoes from our garden.

"What's this?" he asks, eying the table set with candles lit in the center, and the sandwiches I made by my very own self.

"Ta-da! I have Grand Gestured you," I announce.

"Ah. The thing you told me about in your romance novels where one of them does something bold to prove their love?"

My heart stutters at hearing him say the word *love*. "Yep. Have a seat."

He does and takes a bite while I pour him a glass of wine.

"It's a good sandwich, don't get me wrong, but—"

"No, no. That's not all the Grand Gesture." I pull the plane tickets from my shorts pocket. "I flew to Arizona and broke up with Logan."

He glances at the stubs in my hand and then back at me in disbelief. "Today?"

"Yeah."

He scoots his chair back and pulls me into his lap. "That's a damn good Grand Gesture."

"Thank you. Are you going to ask me on a third date now? We could take a walk at the park right now even, maybe..."

Instead of ripping my clothes off and taking me on the table, he is upsettingly gentlemanly about asking me out on Friday, late.

"What are we doing? Netflix and Chill?"

He trails a finger across my cheek. "It's a surprise."

FIVE

IN ANOTHER LIFE, I want to be reincarnated as a cat. Unlike dogs, they don't seem to give a flying rat's ass about anything. That no-fucks-given state of mind is something I can only aspire to attain.

"My pussy is not happy," I say to Charlotte as we relax on blue yoga mats, spending "cuddle time" with finicky felines before cat yoga.

Miss Kitty, a tubby and slightly weather-beaten tabby, eyes me suspiciously from within an empty pizza box a few feet away from where we sit.

Charlotte coos while Tom, a lean black-and-white male with emerald eyes, nuzzles her side, burrowing his cheek against her belly bump.

"It will be tonight." She waggles her brows. "Third date is the charm."

"Please, stop," I say. "This class is supposed to get rid of my stress, not add to it."

I've been teetering on the edge of an epic meltdown for days, and Charlotte assured me we needed this cat class to de-stress and it seems to be working for *her*. Me, not so much. I should have learned from the goats. Felines are not my friends, but I'm hanging onto the hope that some of the anxiety about my date with Austin will melt away once the deep breathing starts.

"You love this. Admit that I have the best ideas."

"It's okay, I guess."

On a scale of one to ridiculous, cat yoga is a solid five. Okay, maybe a six. The adorable setup gets an extra point because Purrific is also a cat-cafe that gives people an opportunity to get to know adoptable cats. They shut down once a week, on Fridays, for yoga classes with the furry felines. Aw. Now I feel like I should take Miss Kitty home with me, even if she loathes me.

"Ten more minutes with your new friends," our instructor, Layla, a lithe blonde with purple streaks in her hair, tells the eight-person class. "Then we'll get started with thirty minutes of exercise."

"Okay, Miss Kitty," I say to the haughty cat eyeing me with disdain, "let's fall in love with each other." I point to Tom and Charlotte, who are in some kind of symbiotic trance of purrs and pets. "This is what I need you to do, so I'm calm for tonight. Or something close to it. You don't have to touch me if you don't feel comfortable. Purrs are acceptable."

Her amber eyes stay focused on me as she hauls herself up and ambles out of the cardboard container, prowling over to me.

"Ah, she understood you," Charlotte says.

"I just need you to climb on my belly or do something relaxing while I'm planking."

Miss Kitty sharpens her claws on my mat to let me know that won't be happening.

"Maybe I'll just say I'm sick and cancel the date."

"You're overreacting, Chloe," Charlotte chastises me. "You did not come this far to back out."

As much as I don't want to admit it, there may be a sliver of uncomfortable truth to Logan's words about Austin being my security blanket. Living with the guy I'm dating is weird, but at the same time, soothing. I don't have to worry about him calling, or *not* calling, because he's right there. I know when he's at work, when he's busy cleaning, when he's gardening, grocery shopping, the list goes on and on. Truth be told, it almost feels like an invasion of privacy. Like I *shouldn't* know his every movement.

On both ends, actually.

Prior to our relationship, whether or not I shaved my legs in my downtime didn't seem important. As long as the task got done before certain events, like spring, it was no big deal. Now, because of the new dynamic where he's free to run a hand down my leg at any given moment, it's top of my to-do list. There's no mystery, no privacy, and it feels like that could be a stumbling block for a couple whose relationship legs are wobbly like those of a baby doe.

"I'm thinking I need a new place so I don't stifle our blooming relationship," I confess.

"Even though I think you're skirting the real problem, I actually agree with you on not living with him," she says.

"Really?" I avoid asking what the real problem is, because I've got enough problems.

"Yeah. As you know, I've always thought you needed your own place." She strokes Tom's back, while Miss Kitty returns to her pizza box. "It's a lot of pressure already, and where is your room to breathe?"

"Maybe Logan is right. Maybe Austin is the comfortable choice and I don't want to admit it?"

"How so?"

"Well, I kind of know everything about him. And him with me. So we don't have to go through the awkward discovery phase."

"Isn't that a good thing?"

"Is it?"

"You know, you remind me of some of these cats."

"Aloof and majestic?"

"No. Looking for a forever home yet running to hide when the opportunity presents itself."

I look over at Miss Kitty, who has now moved into an empty puzzle box near a brunette who is trying to coax her out of her shell.

"She's so cute." I hear the woman say to Layla. "One day, I'm going to take her home when she's ready."

Miss Kitty stares at her, but stays away. Charlotte's right, of course. I'm probably looking for an opportunity to bolt. And when yoga starts, I breathe out all my worries and chant a mantra in my head that I will not run and hide. I will see this through.

THE PERFECT SURPRISE doesn't exi—

"*Sorpresa*," Austin drawls, opening the back door to the restaurant where he works.

"What is this magic you're speaking?"

The chilly air of the kitchen cools my heated skin

as I step inside and look around for a fire extinguisher to douse the blaze he just ignited in my panties.

"It means 'surprise' in Italian."

Despite my many attempts to kiss it out of him, Austin remained mum about our date, so I glance around, trying to figure out the surprise. Our date is late, past eleven, and I'm uncertain what the plan is here. The restaurant is closed and all the employees have left for home.

"Are we going stargazing after you take care of business?"

"Come with me." He laces his fingers in mine and leads me past the stainless counters and cooking equipment through the swinging door into the dining area.

Ah.

A few feet from where we stand is a linen-draped table with one lit candle casting a soft glow next to an open bottle of wine.

"You're so romantic," I say.

"Voglio cucinare con te," is his perfect response.

I mean, I have no idea what he said, but does it matter when it's spoken in another language by those lips?

"Yes," I say. "Whatever that means, the answer is yes."

He smirks. "It means, I want to cook with you. I

thought we could make a tasting menu of dishes I plan to serve once this place becomes mine—officially."

"As long as you keep talking like that, I'm up for anything. And I do mean anything."

His dark eyes flare with sultry heat. "Oh, yeah?"

I tiptoe my fingers up his chest. "Mm-hmm."

"I'll remember that." He dips his head to tantalize me with a sensual brush of his lips against mine to murmur, *"Mi ecciti così tanto.* You really turn me on."

"Same, Chef, same," I whisper back.

My forehead is blessed with a kiss and then he leads me back into the kitchen, where I lean against the counter as he puts on an apron over his dress shirt and jeans. The perfection here is ridiculous. He cooks, he cleans, and he's a damn good kisser.

"I had no idea you spoke Italian." Relief settles in, easing some of the earlier worries, because apparently we don't know everything about each other. All this time, I've thought I knew him so well, and do I? Yes, I know things about his personality, but I didn't know *this*. And what a wonderful thing to find out.

He glances over at me as he hustles around the kitchen retrieving various veggies, oils, and seasonings. "If you're going to work in a restaurant, it's important to speak at least the basics of a few languages. My boss is Italian, and I loved listening to him. So I took some online classes in my spare time apart from what he's taught me."

He explains he pre-prepared some of the dishes earlier to save time and I listen as he tells me about what we'll be sampling—risotto *alla milanese*, panzanella, cacio e pepe, and of course, pizza.

"Sounds amazing. I know it will be delicious."

He preheats the industrial oven to warm the samples and then removes a white towel from atop a large bowl and sprinkles a dusting of flour on the counter and hands me an apron.

"It's time to put those hands to use."

Clearly he means the ball of dough he drops before me and not a handjob. Bummer. But not really, because then he says, *"Ho una fantasia. La vuoi sentire?"*

My bones turn to putty as I tie the apron over my wrap-around dress. I'm going to melt right here in this kitchen and he'll have to mop me up off the tiled floor. "That sounds like a question, and again, whatever it is, the answer is yes."

"Translation: I have a fantasy. Do you want to hear it?"

My hands halt on tying. "Damn straight, I do," I manage to get out.

His eyes sweep over me from head to toe. "One

day I come home from work, and you're in the kitchen, wearing nothing but an apron, and I spank you for being such a naughty girl, and then I tie your hands and fuck you right on the table."

Oh, my. Fire rushes through my veins and I'm still not used to this unabashed side of Austin with me. I swallow and try to answer, but his dirty words have caused a brain malfunction.

"You're blushing." He trails a finger along my cheek. "*Mi piace stare con te.* I like being with you."

"I like being with you too." As our gazes stay locked, so many things I like about him are on the tip of my tongue when the oven beeps, breaking us from the spell we're under. "I guess we should get back to cooking?"

And we do. Within thirty minutes, we have an array of samplers on the table, ready to devour.

He pulls out my chair, and when I'm seated, leans in to whisper, "I hope it tastes as good as you do."

Best date ever. We have a nice dinner, envisioning together the little changes he wants to make in the restaurant.

"I think maybe the bar should get moved over there, so it's more of a focal point." He points with his fork to the empty rear wall.

"Yeah, that's a great idea. Oh, if you do that, maybe you should also change the lighting…"

He arches a brow, considering my suggestion. "What if it was those little twinkly light-thingies? They're LEDs, so they're efficient, but they also add atmosphere."

"That would be perfect."

Just like this date. We continue talking about the changes as the food disappears. With the candlelight dancing on his face, I am enraptured by everything he says, cataloguing the way the fork slides past his lips, the way his brow pulls together as he thinks. The way he looks at me, like I'm more valuable than diamonds, when I make a suggestion.

"Maybe you could paint some Italian scenery on that wall?"

"I'd love to. It will be a very swoony atmosphere."

Just like the one I'm feeling now. But still…

"Hey, Austin?"

"Yeah?"

"Can we third-date in the traditional manner now?"

"God, yes."

SIX

IT'S SEXIN' time. Finally. After all my wishes and fantasies, Austin is about to have sex with me. *Me.* This is it. This is the moment I've dreamed about for so many days and nights. I'll finally know what it's like to be with him.

And now I don't know if I can handle it. The pressure is crushing me beneath its weight.

What if it's a letdown?

What if it's *not* is the scarier outcome.

My brain can't comprehend that this is finally happening, but my body is ready and begging for it. In a haze of deep kisses, we paw and grasp our way to Austin's bedroom, shedding shoes and inhibitions along the way.

His kisses and moans are drug-like, making me feel higher than a mountain of gummies. With no frightening bacon-leg side effects. Well, maybe a few. I do feel weak in the knees.

When we reach the middle of his room, he stops and wrenches his succulent mouth away from mine.

"I need to slow down, and savor you," he says. "I've waited a long time for this and I don't want to rush it."

A little fearful I'll chicken out if things don't happen in a hurry, I rise on tiptoes and slide my hand around his neck, into his hair, and pull him closer. "I'm okay with fast."

"Ah, God," he says, grinding his hardness into me. "I want you so badly, more than anything, but I want to take my time with you more."

With nimble fingers, he releases the tie at my waist holding my dress together, and slides the material off my shoulders. It flutters to the floor, revealing my black panties and bra. The good ones, obviously.

His dark eyes devour my body. Goosebumps race across my skin when he trails his finger along my bra, tracing the lace edged deep v, dipping his finger in the valley between my breasts.

"You're beautiful," he says, unhooking the front clasp.

He palms my breasts, and I let out a loud moan when he sucks on a nipple, grazing his teeth along the stiff peak, nibbling and biting. When he's loved on both until they ache with desire, he inches down, covering my abdomen with wet, hot kisses. My hands tug at his hair as he nips each hip, and then slides my panties off.

He places another kiss on my mound—which is a word I'm unsure if I like, but it's used frequently in romance novels—and slides his tongue along the seam.

Don't get me wrong, I am all for the oral sex, but...

"God, that feels good," I say before a groan slips out, because what he's doing feels phenomenal.

But as I was saying before he started eating me like I'm the last meal he'll ever get, I want to reciprocate.

He grips my ass, pulling me flush with his face, licking and sucking, but I shimmy away in a daze of lust.

"What's wrong?" he asks.

"Nothing. It's my turn to give to you. And you can't say no."

He rises, and with quick movements, sheds his clothes until he's standing before me naked.

"Wow," I murmur, admiring the lean, muscular body I've fantasized about so many times.

My eyes dive into all the nooks and crannies of his etched abs, lingering on the chiseled muscles on his hips which showcase the ginormous cock pointing straight at me. Even his balls are beautiful.

I drop to the floor, one knee and then the other, and glance up at him as I kiss the tip, licking the salty pre-cum with a slow drag of my tongue.

"Christ," he grits out. "Keep looking up at me." He fists my hair around his hand, so I have no curtain to shroud me. "I want to see you take me in your pretty mouth."

The look on his face—raw hunger—mesmerizes me as I slide his thick length past my lips and take him deep down my throat. His eyes fall shut for a second, and then open to watch me suck his velvety thickness. I've never enjoyed giving a blowjob as much as this one. There are no worries whether I'm performing to the best of my abilities, because he's very vocal about his pleasure.

"Your mouth is so hot." He bucks his hips, pulling my hair just enough to make my scalp tingle and want more. "Fuck. So good, Chloe."

He fucks my mouth, and everything feels right as I suck and pump him until his thighs quiver. He lets out a primal groan when I reach up to fondle his balls, and then he pulls away from me with a curse.

"It feels too good. If you don't stop, I'll come."

Before I have time to beg him to do just that, I'm pulled to my feet and his lips are on mine in a ravishing kiss that makes every erotic tale I've read seem like a child's fantasy. And I realize that's what I've had all this time for him. A girlish fantasy that could never live up to this flesh and blood reality.

Tremors rock my body as Austin glides his warm mouth down my neck and we land on the bed in a tangle of limbs.

"Where are the handcuffs?" I ask.

"How do you know about the handcuffs?"

"*Condom*, I said condom," I hastily backtrack.

"We'll discuss this later."

He kisses every inch of my body, unraveling me with his tongue and fingers, finding erogenous zones I didn't know existed until now. Nothing I could have imagined in my wildest fantasies compares to the whisper of his warm breath against my skin, the tug of his hands in my hair, the heavy pants, the feel of his hard body against my softness.

I pull him closer, wanting to do all the things I've spent years pining over in my mind. Wanting this to be as good for him as it is for me. I don't want him to ever forget our first time together. Because I know no matter what happens after this night, I'll never forget it. My greedy lips and hands trail over his body, exploring and reveling in the discovery of spots that make him moan a little louder and pant a little heavier.

My mind photographs all the sexy things about him, saving them to look at later. The sweat on his brow. The tussled hair. The kiss-swollen lips.

Every nerve ending in my body is electrified as he rolls on a condom and settles between my legs. He braces on one arm, looking down between us as he rubs the head of his cock against my entrance. "You're so wet," he says. "I need inside you, Chloe. Are you ready for me?"

Our eyes meet, and I whisper my deepest secret, "I'm scared."

"Me too," he murmurs, holding my hand above my head.

"I want you more than I've wanted anything." I arch my hips and the tip eases inside, stretching and filling me.

"Fuck," he rasps as he slides further into me. "You're so tight."

When he says those words, it turns me on even more. I buck against him, encouraging him to go faster and ease this ache in my core.

"Yes," I pant out. "More. I want more."

He groans and catches his bottom lip with his teeth, taking his time, letting me acclimate to his size, inching deeper until he's rooted to the hilt.

This.

This moment.

I want to memorize it and lock it away. Never share it with anyone. Because it's too good. It's mine and no one else can have it.

He withdraws and my body misses him immediately, but he reads me like a book, thrusting back in with a quick stroke, never breaking eye contact. Need swirls with passion, and I cling to him, scraping my nails down his back, over his ass, moaning out his name as he rocks in and out, over and over.

This is not sex. Or fucking. There's no doggy-style or position that prevents eye contact. This feels like making love. This feels like bliss.

I search his eyes, nearly black now, to see if he's feeling it too. His stare is so intent; there is no mask for me to hide behind. It's as if he can see inside me, right to where I have all my insecurities hidden. And they don't frighten him.

My eyes fall shut as I languish in the connection, in the burn simmering low in my belly, threatening to incinerate me.

"Look at me," he says, pumping faster, creating a delicious friction. "Don't shut me out. I want to see everything you're feeling."

I do as he says, and his hips jerk, driving in so deep I feel him in my soul. In a place I've let no one reach. I feel him in my heart.

"You're going to make me come soon," I say, with quick pants, meeting his thrusts.

"Oh God," he says, jerking faster. "Come on me. I'm waiting for you." The arm braced beside me quivers with the strain of holding back.

My toes tingle and my orgasm looms with every swift stroke. As he pumps into me, our sweat-soaked bodies slide against each other like they were made for each other. As the tightening low in my belly unwinds, I shatter beneath him, leaving the pieces for him to put back together.

"I feel you coming. Jesus," he says, ramming into me with ferocious strokes.

As my orgasm crests, his body shudders, and he releases on a growl. It's the most beautiful thing I've ever seen, watching the pleasure roll across his face like sunlight on a canvas, revealing new things for me to appreciate. The clench of his jaw. The errant lock of hair dropped onto his forehead. The shadow of his thick lashes when he briefly closes his eyes.

When our bodies calm, he stays inside me, sprinkling my face with kisses. My cheeks, nose, forehead, eyes, and lips.

And then he pulls out and heads to the bathroom. After a few minutes, he returns with a towel and cleans me up.

He pulls the covers back on the bed, and drags

me into his arms. I snuggle into him, still feeling him inside me. In the darkness, I ghost my foot along his leg, already replaying everything in my mind. The silence is comfortable, and I watch the shadows cast by the moon, dance along the wall.

"That...that was amazing," he says, tracing lazy eights on my arm.

"Yeah, it was."

I don't know what else to say, because I have no words to elaborate. It was more than amazing. It was perfect, really. All that waiting was worth it. I'd wait centuries to have that again. A lifetime. It was that good. That special.

"Your bed is so comfortable," I say. "It's like a fluffy cloud but firm enough to give good back support. And your sheets are cool. I like cool sheets."

"Thanks, that's kind of what the salesman said. If you ever stop making pottery, that may be your second calling." I laugh and he pulls me closer. "It feels good with you in it. I'm a bed hog, just so you know. So if you find yourself hanging off the edge, it's not you, it's me."

"Good to know." See, I didn't know everything about him. "Did you know King Tut slept in a bed made entirely of ebony and gold?"

"I did not know that." I can hear the smile in his voice.

"Yeah. His servants slept on palm fronds. Sad, right?"

He chuckles, and with my head against his chest, I listen to the steady rhythm of his heartbeat until it lulls me to sleep.

There is no turning back now.

He knows it.

I know it.

We'll never be just friends again.

And all that terror I felt about it?

Gone.

This is what it feels like to have all your dreams come true.

SEVEN

I REALLY OUGHT to know by now that sex soothes my mind, but my anxieties are never really *gone*, just napping. They reawaken and stretch their ugly claws when on my lunch break I spy Lucy and Finn, wearing matching SuperFit gear, sipping celery juice. I'm almost out the door of the smoothie shop, undetected, when I hear Lucy call out to me.

"Chloe, hi."

I'm in that awkward phase of pretending I don't hear her, fiddling with my straw to avoid making eye contact, when she rises from their table by the window and waves her arm. Ugh.

"Chloe," she says again, louder this time.

A stranger taps me on the shoulder. "I think she's trying to get your attention."

Thanks, stranger.

I turn toward the sound of her voice. "Oh, hey. I didn't see you there."

She motions me over, and I force my feet in their direction.

"I see you're making healthy choices," Finn says. "Good girl."

"Well, I had a burger earlier. With mayonnaise." I hold my strawberry smoothie cup up in a passive-aggressive move. "This is my dessert. Extra whipped cream."

"Yum," Lucy says. "Are you working today?"

"Yeah." And then I do the polite thing and ask what they're up to, when really I shouldn't.

"We had a workout, and after this, we're meeting Finn's parents at their lake house. His stepmother and I are going shopping, while the men fish." She gives me a wink and a thumbs-up.

"Sounds super fun."

This should be the end of our conversation, a good place to say "great seeing you" before darting out of the door, but Lucy and Finn proceed to fill me in on their newfound happiness and about Finn's luxurious condo.

"It feels so good to stand up straight," he says. "I swear that tiny house gave me a hunchback."

Lucy rubs her hand down his back. "No, it didn't,

babe. But your new place is a much better fit for you."

"I'm sure it is," I say.

And then my anxieties go full Godzilla stomping through my body, destroying the barricades I'd erected to keep them at bay when Finn says,

"I tried to get Lucy to move in with me, but she thinks it's healthier if we maintain our separate spaces." He drapes an arm on the back of her chair, playing with the ends of her hair. "I guess she's right. Even if I'd rather have her there all the time."

"Well, it's important to have those boundaries in a new relationship, and not be together 24/7," she says, affirming my worries. "It's good to miss me. It makes our time together sweeter. Don't you agree, Chloe?" She realizes her mistake, because hello, I don't have my own place. "Oh. Never mind." She takes a sip of celery juice and changes the subject. "So how are things with you and Austin?"

This interaction with them is outside of my comfort zone. And I decide from this moment on to duck and run if I ever see them again. Screw being an adult. "They're great." I look at an imaginary watch on my arm. "I really have to get back to work. Enjoy your day."

"See you later," she says, giving Finn starry eyes.

Outside, I dump my smoothie in the trash because now there are a million butterflies in my stomach. Back at work, my anxieties wrap their fingers around my throat until I feel like I'm choking, so I try to soothe myself with some second opinions on the internet. Big mistake. The internet experts agree dating a roommate isn't ideal. Time apart is crucial to fledgling couples who previously lived together as roommates, they say.

I take a deep breath and remind myself we've gone from zero to sixty and really, I'm more of a *Driving Miss Daisy* type of gal, so it's natural I have these fears.

When I finally come home from the long-ass day at It's Clay Time, firing one million dishes between checking kids in for birthday parties, wanting nothing more than to soak my tired feet in the tub while listening to the *Talk Like a Lady* podcast, Austin is lounging in the living room with his guitar.

For a beat, I linger in the doorway, unsure of how this works. Everything has changed, and I don't do well with change. Yes, we had phenomenal sex last night and cuddled after, but where are our boundaries? Am I supposed to drop my stuff off and hang out with him?

Am I supposed to ask?

Is he feeling awkward about us?

How long before he feels trapped and suffocated?

God, it's over and it hasn't even begun.

The questions I have no answers for keep coming, and I lurk in the doorway like a creep overthinking until he looks up and says, "Hey, there's food in the fridge. I picked up Thai fried rice."

He looks happy to see me, so that's good. "Yum. Thank you. I'm starved."

In an Oscar worthy performance, I paste a smile on my face and cross to the living room like I'm not freaking out on the inside.

"I didn't know if you had plans for the night, but I started a free trial of Showtime, so if there's a series you wanted to see, we've got a week's worth of binging available."

Well. Okay. That was easy. My pulse slows a bit and I can breathe. I'm just being my usual overanalyzing self.

"I've actually got a short list of possibilities," I tell him.

My statement is in direct contradiction to the web wizards who said if you're going to date a roommate, it's important to go out and not fall into the trap of staying in and watching Netflix. In my defense, it's not Netflix we'll be watching, and I've been angling for a Showtime password for some time. *The Tudors* looks amazing, and Austin can enjoy my fact-checking in real time.

I drop my bag on the couch and let my hunger lead me to the fridge. So far, so good. I only feel a smidge awkward. Should I have kissed him before bounding toward the dinner he offered?

The lines have crossed until they're a tightrope and I've never had good balance.

Why is life so hard? Can't I just have amazing dick without all these rules and complications?

He follows me into the kitchen and drops down at the table, guitar resting on his knee. "Wanna hear what I've been working on?"

"Do you even have to ask?" I pull out the container from the fridge and pop it in the microwave. "You're going to serenade me while I eat? Swoon."

It's difficult to multitask flirting with a nervous breakdown, but I'm succeeding.

He blows me away with, "I wrote it for you."

My heart somersaults in my chest. "Really? No one's ever written a song for me."

"Yes, they have."

I grab a fork from the drawer. "No, they really haven't."

"I have a confession."

"What?"

When the microwave dings, I gather my food and join him at the table.

"The song on the camping trip...that was about you too."

"The moon," I whisper. "You wrote that for me?"

He nods and gives me a sheepish grin. "Yeah. Is that creepy?"

I laugh a little. "Not at all. I still remember it, the line about history repeating itself, and I remember wanting it to be about me."

"You said why couldn't a guy give you the moon and I don't know"—he shrugs—"I couldn't stop thinking about it."

I feel like I'm *on* the moon, weightless and in uncharted territory, when I rise from my chair and show him what I'm feeling with my lips.

His hand clasps the back of my neck as he takes the kiss deeper, into depths I've never been.

When I'm drowning in desire, we come up for air.

"I could kiss you all night," he says.

"I'd let you, but I want to hear my song."

He swats my ass, and I move back to my seat, feeling more of the anxiety dissipate. A soft melody fills the kitchen as he strums the cords with a flick of his fingers. It starts out slow and sweet.

He sings about meeting a girl prettier than he's

ever seen (Me!) and needing to see her (I'm so lucky!) and wondering what she's doing (Admiring you, big fella!) and driving in his truck to her house. (Huh. Huh?)

You see, she's across town. (Anxiety alert.)

While I try not to choke on my rice, because my throat is closing, his raspy voice sings the chorus.

Is she thinking about him while she's asleep in her bed, miles away. (Miles away?)

Does she miss him when they're apart, like he misses her? (Oh my God, Lucy was right.)

He strums the last chord. "That's all I have for now."

Thank God. And I don't mean that in a bad way, just in an I-may-hyperventilate-if-he-continues kind of way.

"It's beautiful."

"It's a work in progress."

Like me. If I don't get this out, I might die.

"Will you still want to write songs for the live-in girlfriend? Do we need to preserve more mystery? How do we newly date and shack up at the same time?"

He tilts his head. "I think—"

"How long do we maintain separate bedrooms? Most people date and then decide to move in together. We skipped right over that part, Austin.

How much time do we spend together on a daily basis?" My mini-spiral about what to do continues. "These are important things to think about since we spend all day, every day together."

"I don't know the answers," he says and probably thinks he's ended it when he adds, "but, we'll figure it out."

But it does not end there.

It continues for me in the bedroom as I slip into more comfortable clothes. My paint-stained tee and frayed cotton shorts I've worn a million times in front of him? I put them on, look in the mirror, and promptly take them back off. Normally, I wouldn't think twice about my lounging clothes, but now that we're dating, it's a different story. My pink tank and black yoga shorts are less comfy, but sexier. When I pad into the living room, Austin is in his usual position on the couch, so I plop down beside him and rest my feet beside his on the coffee table.

"Ready?" he asks.

"Yeah."

The thoughts holding my mind hostage make it difficult to enjoy the show. The royalty on the screen might as well be speaking gibberish.

But then! My phone buzzes and when I check it...

A notification reads, "Congratulations! Your Kickstarter has been fully funded."

"Oh my God," I breathe out.

"What?" Austin looks over at me.

"My Kickstarter is fully funded. I have the money to rent a space. I can buy a kiln. I can quit my job!"

His eyes light up and he steals what little breath I have left with a celebratory kiss. "That's awesome," he says when he pulls away. "How did you get it funded so fast? The last time we checked, you still needed almost half."

"I have no idea."

I click into the app and scroll through the donors. They all have distinctly MC-like monikers.

"Frog, Rooster, Glock, Scar, Hawk, Snake-Eyes, Shorty, Coco..." Either Dune is involved, or Disney.

Austin chuckles, looking over at my phone as I keep scrolling. "*Coco?* Yeah, I think it's safe to say Dune's friends hooked you up. That's cool. They're good people."

"Yeah."

I send a text to Dune.

Three Things:

1. ***You're amazing.***
2. ***Your friends are amazing.***

3. **_THANK YOU!_**

He responds right away.

No thanks needed. I won a good bet. Finally got my house back, and funding from half the club!

I thank him again and add a barrage of hearts and crying emojis. He reminds me about incorporating, and I promise to follow up with him. And then I can't stop smiling because I'm going to have my own business. Like a real one, with a sign and everything.

I toss my phone back in my purse and snuggle into Austin's side, ready to enjoy the show, even if the worries about us are still front and center. I can do both.

Business-ladies are very good at multitasking.

EIGHT

IF I TOLD you what I'm doing, you wouldn't believe it. Even I don't believe it.

Thank God, I have a village to help raise me, and Charlotte is along for the ride.

Dune's motorcycle roars into the parking lot of Handle Bar, where Charlotte and I stand waiting to talk with one of his friends about a rental property for Mae'd. When he contacted me about it, he assured me there's no nefarious activity at the place, so here I am. It's Friday night, and after a week of sex so fantastic I can barely walk followed by worries so heavy I can barely breathe, I snagged Charlotte while Austin works a double shift to meet up with Dune and his friend to get more details about the space, which also includes an apartment above it. That's all he told me when he texted earlier, because he's vague like that.

His booted feet eat up the ground until his leather-vested chest is in front of us. "Hey. Thanks for coming. Hopefully, this works out. I think you're going to like this place."

"Fingers crossed," I say.

"Mine too," Charlotte says.

He opens the door for us, and we follow him into the rowdy bar. The regulars give us waves and chin nods as we pass through the crowded space.

"Does this count as bringing a baby into a bar?" Charlotte asks as we weave through the leather vests.

"They have food too, so technically you can say it's a restaurant."

"Good point," she says. "Oh, look. It's Jell-O-wrestling night."

"Ah," I say, remembering my brief career in the ring—well, pool. "Good times."

We follow Dune to a table in the corner where he finally stops in front of a silver-haired woman.

A small woman who is a big cheater.

Bev.

Aka Jell-O Champ.

"Told Bev you were looking to rent a space, and she's got one," Dune says. "I'll let you two talk, and

I'm going to go say hi to my brothers. I'll be back in a few minutes."

Bev sips a Heineken, eyeing me over the glass bottle.

"Thank you for agreeing to meet up to discuss this," I say. "Dune didn't give me a lot of details."

"It's in a prime location," she says, getting right down to business. "Just off Pearl. I've been renting it out for years to a woman who sold wind chimes and dream catchers to launder drug money. She's moving to Miami, so it will be available in a month or so."

"Oh, okay. Prime location is good." Ideally it won't come with any phone taps.

She pulls her phone from between her breasts to show me pictures of the place, and it's perfect. Large and airy, with good lighting, built-in shelves, and wood floors. The apartment is a good size too, with a modern kitchen and large rooms. It even has a big claw-foot tub in the bathroom. But then she tells me the price, and my excitement deflates as quickly as it ballooned. I'd be cutting it close, considering I still have to have a kiln installed.

"I think it's out of my price range. I'll need to talk to my financial guy." Dune. It's Dune.

"I've got interest from a few other people, so I don't really have a lot of time to give you to think." She puckers her cigarette-wrinkled lips, studying me.

"I'd be willing to cut you a deal on the price, since you're family."

"Really?"

These people are truly my people. I'm on the verge of hugging her for her generosity until...

"On one condition. Let's have another showdown in the pool. You beat me, and I'll work with your budget, pending your finance guy's approval."

Charlotte's eyes widen as they bounce between us.

I'd just like to say, that's nice and all she's willing to take less, but how many families make you Jell-O wrestle for a discount?

"Give me one second, please."

She arches an intimidating brow at me. "Scared I'll win again?"

"Not at all. Just need to discuss the space with my friend."

I smile politely and pull Charlotte away to an empty space behind a cactus.

"What should I do? That place is gorgeous. I mean...it has a claw-foot tub. That's my dream tub. I could really enjoy *Talk Like a Lady* in that thing."

I'm expecting her to tell me not to risk my life over a tub, but she says, "How can you *not* do this? I feel like this is going to be a cool story to tell my kid one day. Imagine their wonder when I tell him or her how Aunt Chloe Jell-O wrestled her way into the perfect property. You must. Right?"

I peer through the prickly arms of the cactus over to where Bev sips a beer. "She's a wily woman for her age, though. What if I lose? It will be doubly disappointing."

"Don't count yourself out of the Jell-O war. You're wily too. I was in awe of your lotus move at cat yoga," Charlotte says. "I mean, not to be rude, but... she's at least forty years older than you and the size of my arm. How did you not win last time?"

I park a hand on my hip. "She cheated. That's how. And Jell-O is more slippery than ice."

"True. True. Okay, so, what are you going to do?"

"I really need an exit plan for Austin and me. If things go south, one of us would have to move out. And that's so much pressure."

She smiles. "I think you know what you have to do then. Are you ready to rumble?"

And that's how I end up yet again wearing a borrowed one-piece swimsuit, standing in line for a rematch with Bev.

Charlotte, Dune, and a bevy of bikers gather round the blowup pool filled with lime Jell-O as Bev and I take our places on opposite sides of the pool.

"You got this, Chloe," Charlotte shouts with way too much glee. "Woo-hoo!"

When the referee blows his whistle, this time I'm prepared for her sneak attack and opt to dive into the gooey mess instead of trying to stand in the slippery concoction. I hit the bottom with a thud. Of course, I planned to swim across, grab her by the ankles like an incognito shark attack, but you can't really swim in Jell-O.

But you can slide.

And I do, all the way across the length into the opposite side. It bows out and pops me back like a boomerang.

"Wook wout," it sounds like Charlotte says because of the Jell-O in my ears.

"What?" I ask.

It doesn't take a genius to figure out she meant "look out" as Bev bounds onto my back, wrapping her leathery arm around my throat. She's like a monkey I can't shake off.

I stumble and slide, but she stays latched on to me.

"Give it up, girl," she says. "You can't beat me."

This is *not* how family acts. If my mouth weren't filled with Jell-O, I'd tell her that. When she pins me in the corner, Charlotte gasps.

Bev's underestimated the level of my anxiety and just how much I want that place, though. And also how many sex moves I've learned in the last year. I buck my hips and circle them, pushing back —like the reverse cowgirl the other night with Austin—and tangle my legs with hers until I flip us over.

She's as shocked as I am as I stare into her hazel eyes. The crowd cheers as she tries to wiggle away and I struggle to hold on to her. The ref starts counting and I'm ready to celebrate my victory when she gives it one last go and kicks me square in the vagina. Hard.

An oomph rushes out of me, and I lose my grip.

"That was not nice," I say as she grabs my hair and drags me beneath her tiny self.

"Never said I was."

And that's how I lose to an old lady yet *again*. Cheater.

Charlotte and Dune help me out of the pool as Bev pumps her arms like she just won a gold medal.

"You did good," Dune says.

"You really did," Charlotte agrees, handing me a towel. "That move you did in the beginning where you slid across the pool was so impressive."

"Whatever." My goopy shoulders slump. "You don't have to lie to me. Next time, I'm cheating."

"I like that you've accepted there will be a next time," Charlotte says with amusement in her eyes.

After Bev finishes her victory lap in the Jell-O

pool, she climbs out and walks over to us. "Call me tomorrow. We'll do that deal we talked about."

"But I lost."

"Maybe so." She pats my arm. "But you're family."

Charlotte squeals, and I do too as I wrap Bev in a hug. She can kick me in the vagina any day. I have an exit plan.

"IT'S weird to be out with you and Austin as a couple," Charlotte whispers to me as we trail behind Austin and James on our first double date. It's a real relationship-y thing to be doing, which my friend clearly recognizes. "Do *you* feel weird?"

"I always feel weird."

And that's the truth. I'm not sure how to navigate this new territory of us as a couple with friends. It's James's birthday, so we've decided to have fancy drinks out on the town. He's a bit of an introvert and hanging out with Charlotte's bestest friends for his birthday is as much of a party as he wants. I'm delighted to show them the speakeasy, seeing as Logan is out of town.

As we approach the hidden entrance, I can't help but wonder for a moment if it's rude to take them to the place where I had my first date with someone else. But I had a really fun night there. And really delicious drinks. So why wouldn't I want to share another fun night there with my friends?

It's not like I'll never go to the tapas place again because we once had dinner there. It's silly to avoid places you loved because you're no longer with the person who introduced you to it.

Right?

Right.

At the door, I do the special secret knock, and we're ushered inside and back in time.

"Ah, I love this," Charlotte says.

"Yeah. This is cool," James says, checking out the suspender-clad servers moving about the area.

We find an empty table near the jazz band and James pulls Charlotte into his lap. "How are you feeling, mama?"

"Good," she says, dropping a sweet kiss on his nose.

I take my cue from them and slide onto Austin's knee.

"Hey there," he says with a grin, but also surprised by my transition into his bubble. "Can I ask why you're sitting on me?"

I drape my arm over his shoulder. "We're a couple now."

"Yes, but—"

"Don't fight it."

He doesn't, and to his credit, wraps his arm around me, even though he seems confused by my intrusion.

But really, I don't know what I'm doing sitting here either. I just know I like having the chance to act outwardly the way I've felt inside forever.

But...

I don't want to do the thing Lucy did at the bachelorette party, being the snake to his Britney. So I end up just sort of perching on him, a single butt-bone on his thigh, which is not comfortable for either of us, or satisfying in any way.

A tall guy with biceps bursting out of his striped shirt takes our order and as Charlotte asks for a virgin mint julep, I scoot off Austin's lap into my own seat. Even if that didn't go over well, no one seems to notice. Our conversation flows, and I want to pinch myself, because I'm on a dang double date with *Austin* as my date!

It's exciting. But as the night goes on, I realize there are just a hundred ways I don't know how to bridge the transition.

For example, it's funny that in moments like these, where we're laughing and having fun, I used to say "God, I love you guys" when we were hanging out and agreeing on stuff all the time, but now that we're together, I'm scared to go anywhere near the word. When Austin makes a corny joke and everyone groans, usually I'd say, "This is why we love you."

Can't say that shit anymore.

Oh, well. Maybe things will get easier. If not, at least I have an exit plan.

NINE

*MEET **me at 4PM by the little tree in the courtyard of Artopia. I have something planned that will make you happy.***

"Your guy is so romantic," Anna gushes while we swoon over the fragrant bouquet of wildflowers just delivered to me at It's Clay Time. "You kind of have the perfect life. You know that, right?"

"My life is far from perfect," I say, lifting the crinkly wrapper surrounding the bushel of flowers to take a whiff. "But how awesome someone thinks it is."

With a dazed grin, I tuck the typewritten card back in the attached envelope. Austin never let on he was planning something special today. Before I left for work this morning, he said he was pulling a double shift and wouldn't be home until late tonight.

Which is the norm these days. I'm still trying to build a bridge over the troubled transition-waters, but we're like two ships passing in the night.

"Seriously? Let me count all the ways it's perfect." She counts off her fingers. "You've got a booming side business and a genius side-side business. A hot guy planning romantic dates and sending you beautiful flowers. You've got wonderful friends and great hair. How is that not perfect? When Charlotte makes new mommy friends, I'd like to apply for the position of your new bestie, so maybe some of your good luck will rub off on me."

That's super sweet. She thinks I'm worthy of best friend status. My hair is nowhere as shiny as Lucy's, but it is shinier than hers, and...

"Wait." I tilt my head and ask the thing I don't want to know the answer to, "What do you mean by new mommy friends?"

My question earns a slight side-eye from her. "You must've heard about this... Most people start hanging with other mothers once they have babies. It's the way of the universe. Like a baby cult. My sister is the perfect example. Once Carter was old enough to walk, she started making playdates with other mothers she met at the park. Socialization and new stuff in common and all that."

"Ah."

She moves away to help a customer, leaving me to deal with the disarray she innocently caused in my mind.

Her words haunt me on the drive to Artopia, spooking me into a panic. In all the scenarios I've worked through my head, Charlotte finding new mom friends who would oust me wasn't one of them. I mean, no one can replace *me* in Charlotte's inner circle. I'm sure she'll make mom friends, but they won't have our history or connection.

Right?

They haven't held her hair back while she hugged the toilet after she smelled eggs frying or dried her tears over her jeans no longer zipping. They certainly didn't help pick out the cute maternity wardrobe she now owns or purchase a pair of mom jeans at her request just so she wouldn't feel alone. And they absolutely didn't plan the Baby Is Coming Pinterest board. They haven't spent hours with Charlotte picking out the travel theme to paint on Baby Charlotte's walls—because this baby is going places—nor will they have painted those scenes for Baby Charlotte to study.

But they will have the one thing I don't possess. Shared experience with babies.

I can picture it now. They'll all be rocking babies,

patting their puffy diapered bottoms, and I'll be just rocking.

Oh God.

What if Baby Charlotte doesn't like me?

That's a scenario I don't want to even consider at this moment. Just because cats don't like me doesn't mean a tiny human won't.

As I park in the crowded lot of Artopia, I make a mental note to check into one of those fake pregnancy bellies so I can go through the rest of this pregnancy with Charlotte. Bet none of the new interloping mom friends would do *that* for her.

Even better than a mental note, I send a text to Charlotte, because there is no time to lose when other mothers are waiting to encroach on friendship territory.

Random thought...should I get one of those sympathy bellies to commiserate with you? So we can have a lived experience?

The fuck is wrong with you? Do it immediately. I need someone else to feel my pain. #bellybesties

Well, it's settled. Phew. My world settles now that I have a plan. Sunlight warms my shoulders as I cross the parking lot to the expansive courtyard full of artsy people lounging on blankets, enjoying the summer afternoon, as I scope out the place looking for Austin.

Across the lawn, next to a maple sapling, I spot glossy, dark hair being played with by the summer breeze. While his back is to me, I slow to a snail's pace to ogle the long legs and sculpted calves leading up to a muscular ass. It's grabbable, so I do, because I can do things like this now.

"Hi," I say, palming a handful of posterior deliciousness.

And then I freeze. The butt cheek I'm holding, while a similar ratio of squishy and firm, doesn't belong to Austin. Oh no. Oh no, no, no. It belongs to the last person I expected to see.

Logan.

I slow blink. They, uh, *do* look alike.

"Hey, you." His baby blues twinkle with mirth. "Is that the new handshake? Can I shake yours?"

I jerk my cheating hand away from his buttocks. "I'm so sorry. I thought you were..." Seems exceptionally cruel to finish that sentence the way I meant to, so I shift to, "Gone. What are you doing here? I thought you were in Texas."

"I cancelled some tour dates to fly home and see you."

Birds trill, filling the silence between us until I finally find my voice to ask, "Why?"

"To woo you." He looks at the hand now resting on my throat, because I think I swallowed my tongue and cannot speak. "I know you're dating Austin, but I still don't see a ring. And I don't feel like I had time to properly address things before I left."

Maybe I didn't break up with him correctly? And maybe it's time to consider a malpractice suit against the internet experts.

"Well, I wouldn't think wooing would be wise," I say gently.

"Say that three times fast."

I smile. "Logan, I think—"

"Please, just let me do this," he interrupts and then lets out a sigh. "I won't woo you. Okay? I reserved two spots for a Bob Ross paint-along and it's a shame for them to go to waste."

Things click into place as I stare at him, dumbstruck. Meet him by the little tree because he has something that will make me happy. Happy little trees. He knows about my Bob Ross girlhood crush, and oh, no!

I'm being Grand Gestured by the wrong guy.

It's a storybook grand gesture, too, something you'd read at the end of a novel, from the guy you expect to get the girl.

But I'm the wrong girl...and he's not the right guy.

"The bouquet," I whisper. "They're from his paintings aren't they?"

He nods, and I briefly close my eyes. Wooing is making me woozy. This is overwhelming—so thoughtful—and utterly wrong.

I broke up with him out of the blue, and maybe he just needs this closure to move on from me. I can't fault him for trying. From experience, I've had breakups where everything was wrong and it still shocked me they ended things. So it's understandable he's having trouble letting go of what he thinks is someone who is perfect for him.

"Please?" he says. "It's only an hour."

What kind of asshole would I be to walk away right now and not partake? "Okay, let's go paint some happy trees."

We head inside Artopia, a cavernous building with various art exhibits and stores selling everything from hand-painted T-shirts to art supplies. At the directory kiosk, we find the Bob Ross Paint-along directions and follow the signs to the second floor full of conference rooms hosting various events. Logan checks us in with a lanky man who looks like he escaped the seventies. Martin, showing a lot of hairy chest and wearing a gold chain, is a Certified Ross Instructor, and I can't lie...it's so cool.

I don't want to enjoy it as much as I am. Is there a

rule I must have a horrible time to give him closure? Probably, so I only half-smile at the other people already sitting behind easels as we cross the marble floor to the empty wooden chairs in the back row.

Don't judge me, but my pulse races like a pack of thoroughbreds as I finger a rainbow of Bob Ross oil paint tubes. Prussian Blue, Dark Sienna, Titanium White, Alizarin Crimson, Cadmium Yellow, Midnight Black, and Bright Red. At the end of the rainbow sits a golden painter's knife, landscape and fan brush.

Martin instructs us to swirl some colors on the canvas and when we're done, he says, "Today we're painting along to Happy Accident, season eleven, episode thirteen. *The Joy of Painting* wasn't just learning how to paint, it was also therapy for many people. So, I want you to really listen to what he's saying."

A big screen TV mounted on the wall turns on and Bob Ross's unmistakable image guides us into fixing our mistakes. He uses his knife to scrape the paint off his canvas and we do the same.

"We don't make mistakes, just happy little accidents," Bob says.

It's as if he's speaking directly to me. Because this is no doubt a mistake to sit here while Logan smiles at me, swiping away at his canvas. As the tutorial progresses, I can't even look at Logan as we paint a new landscape with a babbling creek and an abundance of happy little trees.

"Ever make mistakes in life? Let's make them birds. Yeah, they're birds now," Bob says in his signature mellow voice.

If only it were that easy.

"Wow, that's a lot of birds. Kind of looks like that movie," Logan teases, peering over at my canvas.

I laugh, but I shouldn't. So I add another bird and let it fly away with the rest.

Bob has so many insightful things to say…

"Trees cover up a multitude of sins."

"Never think about the mistakes you made. Think about the mistakes you will make."

And most important…

"Anytime you learn, you gain."

By the time we're done, I feel a little at peace with some of my happy accidents. There's always a do-over. RIP, devil.

"That was amazing," I say to Logan in the parking lot. "I can't thank you enough."

"Thank you for humoring me. I guess there's no chance for dinner?"

I shake my head. "No. I'm sorry. I really want you to be happy—"

"I get it," he interrupts, opening my door. "I'll be

okay. Maybe we can meet up for coffee before I leave to fly back to Texas?"

"I'll have to let you know." Briefly, I search his face and he doesn't seem devastated...just resigned. Not pleased.

It's a milder version of the look on Austin's face when I arrive home and tell him what happened with Logan.

Austin's definitely not pleased. Doi.

"You can't just immediately start hanging with him like he's Dune." He combs his fingers through his hair, leaving peaks of frustration. "Dune I can handle because I know there was nothing there between you two and he knows what's up. But Logan?"

"I understand what you're saying, but it was unexpected."

"I don't have Lucy over for drinks... Maybe someday, but not when there hasn't been closure."

"I thought I was giving him closure by hanging out with him."

"Were you? Or were you still scared to admit this is real?"

"I'm not scared of anything. I can't believe you still doubt me. I *garden* with you. We have *raised tomatoes* from *seeds* to *sauce*."

He wisely chooses not to point out that he

planted the seeds *and* cooked the sauce. It's the principle.

"I have to run to the restaurant to sign some paperwork." He stares at me for what feels like an eternity before saying, "You understand where I'm coming from, right?"

"Yes," I soothe him, rising up to brush my lips against his.

He leaves to shower and I muse over our first fight. Not an epic fight, nevertheless, his doubts unsettle me. I'm not scared. I'll prove my, um, like? We haven't said the L word yet, but I'll prove it. And I know exactly how I'll do it.

TEN

WHEN FULFILLING A FANTASY, the most important item to have on hand is a fire extinguisher. People would probably think it's required because the fantasy is such a scorcher it needs extinguishing, lest it burn everything to the ground. Welp. They'd be wrong.

Part of Austin's fantasy involved me cooking, so even if it's not my thing, I have to make an attempt to satisfy my man and show him how unafraid I am. Silly me decided the least amount of catastrophe would involve preparing a gourmet salad made with fresh ingredients from the garden, topped with thin slices of delectable pan-seared ribeye. The internet pictures were drool worthy, but it would've been nice if the recipe had mentioned the important detail that when you sear steaks at a high temperature plumes of smoke ensue.

"No need to panic," I say to the empathy baby bump around my waist as every fire alarm in the house shrieks.

For the first time, I fully understand Charlotte's complaints. It's cumbersome and nearly impossible to bend over wearing this heavy silicon. My feet have completely disappeared, but I'm moving, so I know they're still there. Austin won't be home for another thirty minutes, and by the time he arrives, he'll never know what took place before I fulfilled his fantasy. The belly will be gone, and probably never worn again, and all he'll know is the woman wearing nothing—and I do mean nothing—but a newly purchased apron and fuck-me heels cooked a delicious meal that I'll rename blackened instead of pan-seared.

It's just another happy little mistake. Easily fixable.

I pop the cast-iron skillet in the oven and helicopter a dish towel over my head to dispel the cloud of smoke and silence at least the alarm in the kitchen. The deafening chirp persists, so I rush to the patio door and fling it open, letting the breeze dispel the haze lingering above the stove.

As I rest my shoulder against the frame and inhale the clean air, a woman's voice says,

"Oh, dear. You didn't tell me Chloe was pregnant."

In what feels like slow motion, I glance over my shoulder to see two sets of enlarged eyes on my naked ass.

One belonging to Austin.

And the other?

His mother, of course.

My horrified gaze ping-pongs between them. "I'll be right back," I whisper.

Olive musters a wan smile before I slip out the door, and with my Louboutin knock-offs sinking in the ground, hands covering my butt, I waddle across the backyard to the new gardening shed in the yard's corner. Exposing one cheek, I open the door and step inside.

Next to the hoe, I hyperventilate.

I am, in fact, a hyperventilating hoe.

A knock interrupts my death spiral. "Chloe," Austin says. "Can I come in?"

"Do you have clothes for me?"

"Yeah."

I open the door a sliver and peek at him. "Why is your mom here?" It's been well over a year since I've seen Olive. Wouldn't you know today would be the day she makes an appearance?

"She stopped by the restaurant and followed me home to grab some fresh tomatoes to make pasta sauce." He has the audacity to smirk. "I wasn't expecting to see my fantasy when we walked in the kitchen."

"This is not the time to try to charm me. Your mother saw...ugh." I open the door to let him in and awkwardly plop down on a stack of fertilizer.

"It's fine," he says. "Can we discuss the elephant in the room?"

I can't help but smile. "You did not just call me an elephant."

He crouches in front of me and runs a hand over my protruding stomach. "What is this?"

"You weren't supposed to see. I did it for Charlotte. It's a sympathy stomach." I reach under my apron and remove it. "Ah, that feels so much better."

"Do you have any idea how adorable you are?"

"I'm sure your mom would disagree. She thinks your roommate, your *pregnant roommate*, walks around half naked."

He palms my face and his dark eyes search mine. "I told her about us."

I blink. "She knows we're dating?"

"Yeah."

The fact he's shared our status with her so soon surprises me. This is not the timeframe recommended by experts. Wow, it's really official.

"Can I just hide out in here until she's gone?"

"No. You're an adult, remember?"

"A reluctant adult."

He nuzzles my cheek with his nose and whispers against my ear. "Let's do this so we can get to the rest of the fantasy."

As much as I'd rather move into the shed and live off the grid, I know I can't, so I slip on the black shorts and Marshmello tee Austin brought out for me and face Olive in the kitchen to break the news of my terminated pregnancy.

To her credit, she laughs when I explain the belly and when Austin steps out to the garden to gather some tomatoes for her, she shares a secret with me.

"I want you to know, I'm happy you and Austin are giving it a shot. I never told him, but I always thought he was better suited for you than Lucy."

"I never told him, but I thought so too."

"He's always telling me your little history facts." She pats my arm. "I know you'll be good to him."

My heart pounds because she's one more casualty if this doesn't work out. We don't discuss my nakedness because what is there to say? I'm sure Ruth would know. Thank Tattoo Jesus for Olive.

When she leaves, I ponder Austin's words about marrying into a family and how easily she transitioned to the new relationship between us.

Why can't I do that?

I haven't even told Granny Mae it's official yet, much less my mom.

Soon. I'll tell them soon.

IF AT FIRST YOU don't succeed, try again. Or as Granny Mae says, "The first time is practice. The second time is what counts."

While Austin is outside saying goodbye to Olive, the shirt and shorts fly off and I'm back in role-play mode. Bob would be proud of the way I've recreated the scene with no smoke or mom in tow.

"Oh, hi," I say when Austin re-enters the kitchen, bending over with no shame to give him a view of my backside as I retrieve the dish towel I conveniently dropped on the floor.

"Mm," is his sexy response.

I rise from my bendy position and he stalks toward me like a predator, eyes pinned on me, licking his lips. With a swift yank, I'm pulled flush against his chest, and he captures my mouth in a ravishing kiss that quickly descends into my own fantasy being fulfilled.

"I've been dying to fuck you." He rocks his hips into my hand, trailing his tongue over my erratic pulse. "I'm so hard for you."

My self-control snaps, and I unzip his shorts, slipping my hand inside to stroke his velvet thickness. "I want you inside me."

He lifts me and deposits me on the table. "Touch yourself," he says.

Hot and primal fire licks my spine as I spread my legs and let him watch me pleasure myself as he quickly sheds his clothes. His pained groan heightens the sensations and I circle faster when he palms his dick and gives a swift stroke.

I stop the motion of my hand before I come. He steps between my legs and leans down to bite my nipple through the apron's material.

"Should we eat dinner first?" I ask as he rolls on a condom.

"Nope," he says, running the head of his cock through my wetness. "You're all I want right now."

He rearranges me so I'm standing but bent over the table. He gives me a light spank and then another.

"Should we get the cuffs?" I bring up again because even if it's not my thing, it's his.

"No," he says, biting down on my shoulder causing a long moan to release from me. "I don't want to dominate you, Chloe. And I'm not sure I could, even if I tried."

He slides in and I brace my hands on the table, pushing back against him. In the moon-shaped mirror hanging on the wall next to the table, our eyes meet.

His hand snakes around my waist and down to rub my clit as he pumps into me. "I like to watch the expressions on your face when I fuck you."

"I like when you fuck me," I pant out.

"You're so fucking wet."

His moans mingle with mine and he moves faster and faster, lifting my feet off the floor with the power of his thrusts. And then he pulls my cheeks apart and slips the tip of his pinky where no finger has ever entered me. A shiver courses through me, because whoa, I wasn't expecting it to feel so good.

"Does this count as anal?" I say, eyes connected to his reflection. Every romance reader knows anal is the final frontier before an HEA.

"You like that?" He eases in a little further, filling me.

"God, yes," I say.

"Yeah?" His tongue flicks out, wetting his bottom lip. "You want more?"

"Yes," I repeat over and over, greedy for more of this exquisite pleasure.

He pulls out before slamming back into me, a husky groan leaving him.

Tingles start in my toes and soon everything is heightened, and I can't hold back.

"Austin," I cry out, "I'm going to come."

"Fuck, yes. Do it. Come on me," he pleads, bracing his hand on the table. "It's mine. You're mine."

I'm his. Oh, damn. I do. With one swift, tight stroke and a swivel of his hips, my release arches my back, fanning out from my center to every nerve ending like a strike of lightning streaking across the sky. A cascade of bubbles burst along my skin.

His body jerks and my eyes fly open to watch the beauty of his orgasm. He grips my hip so tight, I know it will leave a mark. I like the thought of wearing his mark on my body.

A bead of sweat trickles down the side of his sculptured face and he gives me a lingering kiss before we clean ourselves and finally eat dinner. It's pretty darn good, if I do say so myself. The world needs to recognize when I show my like.

After the kitchen is cleaned, we settle on the couch and I check my voicemail. It's the realtor handling Bev's property.

"Hi, Chloe. This is Sheri. I'm calling to let you know that everything is finalized and Bev is ready to lease the place to you. Call me soon so we can set up a time to discuss things further. Have a blessed night."

I got the place. In my excitement, I immediately call Charlotte on speaker to share the good news with both of my most important peeps at the same time:

"I got the place!"

Austin smiles.

Charlotte asks, "The one with the bedroom above the shop in case things don't work out with Austin?"

She doesn't realize she's on speaker, and Austin's smile disappears.

He can barely look at me as I tell Charlotte I'll call her back.

I know what he's thinking.

"It was a mature decision," I say.

"To have a backup plan?"

It was an exit plan, but semantics.

"Having a backup plan is a grown-up thing. I'm very adult."

"Or you're not grown-up enough to commit."

"We just started dating, Austin. It's a little early to commit to living together."

He says some things that are mean and true.

"You make excuses to excuse what you don't want to admit. You expect this to fail and you want to hide from it."

I say some things that are mean and maybe not true, but feel good to say. "Stop being so holier-than-thou. It's not a good look."

It's not true because everything is a good look on him, but I am not the Comeback Queen.

"I'm going to sleep at the restaurant tonight." He opens the door and tosses over his shoulder, "I'll sleep on the couch because I don't have a backup bed."

He leaves.

I cry.

And then I think about what he said, about my excuses, and I can't make any excuses to excuse them. The word loses all meaning, and I bury my face in Austin's cool sheets and fluffy bed just in case he comes home and I can tell him how sorry I am.

But he doesn't.

This may be the one mistake I can't fix.

ELEVEN

"It's hard to see things when you are too close. Take a step back and look." — Bob Ross

---

THE BEST FRIENDS are those who can tell you you're full of crap without making you feel like crap. It's a fine line and one that Charlotte walks with amazing finesse as I recline in the empty claw-foot tub in the apartment above the new space that will be Mae'd With Love's home.

"I can't believe he didn't know about this place

and I blasted it over speakerphone. Why didn't you tell him about the backup plan? And don't blow smoke up my ballooning butt. You need to be honest with yourself about your reasoning."

I shrug, running a hand over the sympathy stomach Charlotte insisted I continue to provide misery-company with. "I really don't know. It would be so much easier if I had a reason for not telling him. But I don't."

"Dig deeper," she says. "I think you have one, but you don't want to admit to yourself that he was right about everything."

Sometimes I wish she didn't know me so well. She can see through me like glass. "As much as I don't want to admit it, there was nothing untrue in what Austin said. I'm a sham of an adult."

She twists her lips to the side, studying me. "It's more than that. You're cushioning."

"I don't know what that is, therefore, I can't be doing it."

"You are doing it. Now that I think about it, I see it clearly."

"Explain, please."

"Cushioning is when you set up Plan B in case Plan A fails. Chloe"—she sits on the toilet—"those feelings of failure, as much as they suck, are crucial in driving you to put the effort into working toward success."

"What does that mean?"

"You're expecting you and Austin to fail, and you're pre-softening the letdown. When you said you wanted this place in case things didn't work out with Austin, it wasn't because you were going to make sure it worked out. You never thought it would. So you made a pre-emptive strike to lessen the blow."

My brows raise. "Is that what I'm doing?"

"Yeah." She looks very pleased she has diagnosed me yet again. "This place is your cushion, kind of like when someone has another girl or guy waiting in the wings. You chose an apartment for yours instead of making a choice between the two. You're double-dipping."

"Wow, you might be right." If I step back and observe my life from a neutral position, I see Austin isn't the only thing I've cushioned.

"Might be right? You know I am. And can I just say... I know the first baby is really a test run and you don't get things right until like the second or third, but I might be the exception to the rule. After advising you, I'm going to be a phenomenal parent, aren't I?"

"You are going to be exceptional. You should

have seven children. I don't think I realized until now how many backup plans I have in place." I gasp. "Charlotte..."

"What?"

I haul myself into a sitting position. "I even have a backup plan for Mae'd...with Laid. I didn't do it intentionally. It was subconscious, I guess."

"Huh." She taps her finger on her bottom lip, thinking. "Yeah, I guess you do. I'm smart, huh?"

"So smart." I attempt to rise from the tub, but can't. "Listen, this thing is going to have to go or I'll be stuck in the bathtub forever. Will you be upset if I take it off?"

"No." She laughs. "I can't believe you actually bought one of those for me. We're going to have so many great stories to tell this little nugget."

"Probably too many." My lungs expand and I can finally breathe when I unlatch the Velcro and remove my faux belly to step out. We rub our lower backs in the same place at the same time. Synched as only sympathy stomachs can make you.

"Can I have that for James? He needs more empathy for me."

"It's yours. It's really hard to understand pregnancy until you can't see your feet." I clap my hands. "Okay, I need to fix this mess. Because everything is fixable."

I hope.

"Yep," Charlotte says, holding out a hand for me to pull her up. "Can I be honest?"

"Of course."

She doesn't let go when she's standing. "This apartment was kind of my backup plan too. You know, when maybe I feel the need to escape. You can never tell a soul I said that."

"Never. It'll go to my grave." I squeeze her hand. "I'm always your backup plan, no matter where I am."

"Same."

"You won't leave me for new friends? Anna said there's this cult of moms waiting at the park to swoop in and steal you away in their minivans. They're going to have all kinds of things in common with you that I won't. You'll be commiserating over feeding, and diaper blow-outs, and before you know it, you'll be day-drinking with the mommy-and-me's and I'll be making a new Pinterest board of solitaire games called All By Myself."

Her eyes widen to perfect circles. "I can't believe you just said that. You are stuck with me for life, and also whatever place comes after that. This friendship is for eternity. As the cool non-mom, it will be your job to keep me up to date on what's going on in the real world."

"I can do that."

We hug as best we can with her stomach in the way and then she pulls away to ask, "Oh my God, Chloe. Do you have a backup plan for *me*?"

"No." I laugh, releasing her. "Actually, you're the one thing I don't have one for. Although Anna wants to apply, but pinky-swear I didn't let her fill out an application."

She follows me out of the bathroom and into the kitchen where I start whittling away at all of my security nets.

First, I turn off the *monster.com* notifications for art jobs. I have a business of my own to focus on, and it's the only job I really want.

Second, on the drive home I swing by It's Clay Time and officially quit the pottery place to be full-time with Mae'd.

"Obviously, I can never give Mae'd the attention it needs if I'm working full-time," I tell my boss, who accepts my resignation with teary-eyed grace.

"I understand," she says. "I'm so proud of what you've achieved, Chloe. We'll miss you, but this job was just a stepping-stone for your art. I'm always here if you need any advice."

"Thank you. I'm sure I'll need plenty."

We hug, and when I leave, my shoulders feel

lighter and it's not as scary as I imagined to not have the security of It's Clay Time.

At home, I grab my laptop and post a Help Wanted ad of my own…

Seeking part-time help for a booming pottery business—Mae'd With Love.

Qualifications: Must be nice. Everything else is trainable.

(If you don't like babies, no need to apply. We'll have one soon.)

Perks: Featuring the possibility of an on-site apartment for a starving artist like I was a year ago.

Wow, just a year ago I was in my tiny cottage, struggling to live within my means. My life has changed so much in twelve months. It's weird, but the more things I cut loose, the less worried I feel about failure. It's freeing.

Then I take out my phone. My finger hovers over the FriendsOfFriends app while memories of Finn, Dune, and Ryan take a walk through my mind. I laugh a little to myself at the lengths I went to impress them as I open the app and leave a review.

I won't be needing you anymore, but I certainly won't forget you. I didn't find a winner in love via the site, but I ended up

with two really good friends and an amazing Uber driver who shuttled me to and fro between dates. Thanks to you, I realized what I wanted in a relationship, and that what I want matters. Never settle, single people. More than thirty-two million people use dating apps, so don't give up.

Special mention to your marketing department. We had a rocky start, but I'll never look at a loose stone the same way again. So I guess in the end, you did your one job. And did it well.

Peace, love, and happiness to everyone searching for their better half. And if you're lucky enough to find him or her or them, actually be their better half.

And then I close out of the app and press delete.

A tougher one is letting go of the internet dating experts. Although they failed me at most every turn, I do love searching for statistics. Like I did for that review I left on the FriendsOfFriends site. But I don't really need anyone to tell me what I should feel or what I'm looking for in a relationship. I know these things, so I remove all the sites I've favorited and bookmarked on my laptop.

I'm done crowdsourcing my love life. If it's not Granny Mae's advice, I'm no longer interested.

And then I snip the final thread of my safety net. I call Logan. He may not have been a backup plan in the traditional sense of running to him if things failed with Austin, but he would've been easy comfort, I guess.

"Hey," he says.

"Hi."

"You're calling to make sure I understand it's over, aren't you?" He sighs. "I saw it in your eyes."

"Yeah, I don't want you to get the wrong idea about things between us or give you false hope."

"Why is he the better guy for you? I just need to know that part."

"It's not that he's a better man than you are. You're a great guy too."

"Then why?"

How do you explain something like love? "I don't know. I get this ache in my chest when I see him. It's this feeling I can't describe, and it never goes away. No matter how hard I try to ignore it, or redirect it, it just keeps leading me back to him."

We have a good conversation where I tell him it honestly could have been him if I had never fallen for someone else before I met Logan. And that I need to not see him because it's confusing to both of us. And unfair to Austin.

Logan is not Ryan or Dune, and I don't want to pursue a friendship with him if Logan isn't in the same spot as me in his heart. Because I've been in his shoes, and I know there's no chance his outcome will be the same as mine. My heart belongs to another.

"I'm not in the same position in my heart," he says. "So yeah, it's best we don't hang out for now. Someday, but not right now. I appreciate you putting the brakes on it. Because I'll be honest, I'd go as far as you let me. And then an extra mile. And it fucking sucks because I know he would too. I can't even say he's a jerk and you're making a mistake. It would be much easier to say he's an asshole and be angry with you. But I'm not angry, Chloe."

I don't want to do that thing where I say he'll find someone else, because it's been done to me and it really doesn't make you feel any better. Instead I listen as he keeps finding his closure.

Someday I do hope we can be friends, because he's a good guy I don't want to cut out of my life.

"One last time," he says. "You sure about this?"

"Yes," I answer without hesitation.

"Okay. I don't usually give up when I'm going for something I want, but this time I will. Because I want you to be happy too." He chuckles. "But...if things don't work out, give me a call. I kid. I kid."

We spend a few minutes talking about Scarlet Letter's plans for a new album and it's a bittersweet goodbye, but a goodbye, nonetheless. My last safety net is gone. And when I hang up, I finally feel like a true adult.

TWELVE

"Go out on a limb. That's where the fruit is." — Bob Ross

IT'S hard to explore the limb when you're afraid it will snap. I want the fruit, but instead I'm staying in the safety of my nest, where it's safe. Austin and I've been somewhat avoiding each other, making excuses for not being home. Example:

Him: "I'll be working extra late at the restaurant tonight. You probably shouldn't wait up."

Me: "Oh, okay. I have to take care of some things

at Mae'd With Love early in the morning, so I planned to turn in early. Have a good night at work."

Long stare from him before, "See you tomorrow."

Another example:

Me: "I'm painting Charlotte's nursery today so I don't know what time I'll be back. I'm guessing it will be super late because she wants to have Tummy Time and nest with me."

Him: "No problem. I'll be taking over the restaurant soon, so I'm going to stay after closing and run some numbers."

Long pause before I say, "Okay, I'll see you tomorrow."

Today:

Him: "I'm going to add some rows to the garden for fall crops, so I'm going to head to the nursery. I'll be gone awhile. And I want to perfect some recipes later."

Me: "No problem. I have an interview set up, so I'll be leaving soon. I'm not sure how long I'll be gone."

Intense stare and awkward pause before he says, "Good luck. I'll see you later."

HOW LONG DOES it take to ship a damn kiln? That's how long we've been tiptoeing. It's like we've settled into pre-dating, like we've broken up and not addressed it. I miss my cushions. Without anything to protect me, I'm forced to deal with this uncomfortable situation I've created. And I will fix it...after this interview. After I figure out how to fix it. Ideally Tattoo Jesus will bless me with another vision, like the one I received for Laid With Love.

Sigh.

I stare at my computer screen.

It's surreal to think I'm interviewing a potential employee for *my* business. How cool I'm the boss of me. I can never be fired. The devil on my shoulder wanted to consult the internet experts for advice on how to be the best boss ever, but the good girl part said not to dive down that rabbit hole.

And then I cannonballed right into it because technically, it's a different subject than love. Like anything, moderation is the key. And besides, all the advice columns I read were things I already knew from having bosses I liked and disliked. Mostly common sense advice.

Don't micromanage. Obviously.

Be generous with praise. Duh.

Be clear about what you expect from your employees. Mm-hmm.

Develop your workers' talents. Amen.

Actually, if I wasn't done with backup plans, I'd consider becoming an internet expert myself. I have lots of valuable information about dating and life to share with the world. "What Not to Do When Becoming an Adult" would be my first article. Oh, well. Next life.

One of my favorite parts of being a boss is having my very own desk. Bev cut me a deal and included the office furniture in exchange for an arm-wrestling competition that I let her win. Not really. She's got arms of steel. I push away from my desk, and do a quick spin in the plush leather chair because I still can't believe I have an office with professional things. There's a bookshelf in the corner, which I filled with lots of art history books and of course, the Motorcycle Mayhem series that taught me the art of dirty talking, plus an additional leather club chair for when I need meetings with my employees. Which I don't have, but hopefully today is my lucky day.

I blow a kiss to my office and make my way toward the front of the store in case my potential helper arrives early. As I cross the tiles, I see a young woman waiting outside the glass door. She's punctual, so already I'm feeling good, even if my palms are sweating because I've never hired anyone. The boss is probably not supposed to have sweaty palms so I rub them down my sundress. She grins at me and I hide my nervousness behind a smile as I unlock the door.

"Hi, I'm Chloe. Come in."

"Hi, I'm Paisley," the petite brunette with honey-colored eyes says. She extends a small hand tipped with lavender nails. "Thank you for giving me this opportunity to meet with you. I don't have much experience but I'm very nice." Her smile turns into a fascinating frown. "Probably a little too nice. *But* I'm not a pushover. Not that I'm implying you'll try to push me over. I follow the rules. Rules are good."

"That's great." It's odd to be the adult in the room, and I find myself doing my own ramble. "I'm nice too. Or I like to think I am, anyway. I don't really have any rules yet, but I'll probably make a list of a few once I figure out things that need to be rules. Did you know the first law code was written around 1760 BC?"

"I didn't know that. But that's so cool that you do. Are you also a lawyer or something?"

"No, just a history fanatic. I guess it's my hobby."

"I'm a soap carver. I like to carve it into cute little animals. My ex said it was creepy"—she rolls her eyes—"which is why he's an ex."

"It's good you realized that and cut him loose."

"Well, he broke up with me, but I didn't want

him back." She picks at the leather strap of her handbag and says, "Dating is not my thing. I may never date again, actually, because I'm starting to believe the perfect guy isn't out there and wading through the muck isn't worth it. I'll just die alone." She stops talking and her face flushes a vibrant shade of red. "I'm sorry. That was so unprofessional of me to say in an interview. My other part-time job is as a dog walker and the guy is a major grump, but his Yorkies are angels, so if you need a reference, I'm sure he'll tell you I'm an excellent and dependable employee. Also, Yorkies are probably the same as babies in terms of helplessness and cuteness and you really don't even look pregnant except for your hair being so shiny."

I love her. It's like I'm looking at myself from college, and gah, I need to fix this with Austin because what she said about the perfect guy not existing, isn't true.

And when you find him, you better do everything in your power to fix it. Because men like Austin are a rarity. And love will make you shiny.

"It's not my baby, it's my best friend's. If you could give me Mr. Yorkie's number, I'd love to speak with him. But unless you're hiding a criminal past, you're hired."

She squeals. "Oh gosh. Thank you. You won't

regret it, I promise. I'll be the best helper who ever helped."

Once I've written down her boss's information, on my very professional notepad, I grab my purse and walk out with her.

"I'll call you soon," I say, and after goodbyes we go our separate ways.

My first employee. I nearly skip to my car. She's so me, and I can definitely work with me. I've been doing it for a long time. But right now, there's someone else that has been living with me and my anxieties and quirks and filter-free monologues for far too long that I need to stop putting off talking to.

Twenty minutes later, I arrive home and sneak in the door and hustle to my bedroom to grab the box hiding the surprise I made for him. I was saving it for when the new restaurant opened, but now is the time. When I walk in the kitchen, Austin is at the stove, stirring something in a tall pot.

"Can we talk?" I say.

"Sure."

"You were right. I had a backup plan because I was afraid." I place the box on the table. "But I'm not anymore. I made this for you."

His breath catches when he slides the lid off the box and removes a full place setting for his restaurant. Just like he once told me he wanted.

He trails a finger around the edge of the navy plate, studying the delicate vine of flowers circling one edge.

"Did you know when I moved here to Colorado to start college, I was terrified? I moved here to pursue my dream but once I got here, I felt so small next to these enormous mountains. Everything was new, and I didn't know anyone. And then I met a boy at a party, when we both ended up near a planter of bluebells trying to get fresh air."

His dark gaze lifts from the plate and meets mine. "I plucked one and gave it to you because you looked so sad."

He remembers.

"Yeah. I couldn't stop thinking about you after that meeting."

"This is beautiful," he says when he removes the sunshine yellow salad plate glazed with abstract mountains and waves of blue.

"That summer, Charlotte and I went to Boulder Lake. You came along. And you covered me up when my bikini top fell off."

"Guys were staring at you."

I laugh. "I was mortified."

"I was awestruck."

"That's when my crush on you fully blossomed."

He removes the bowl adorned with thick, wavy

stripes. "Remember when you and Charlotte moved in together and hosted a Christmas costume party? You wore a robber costume and served signature drinks named for us, and they were perfectly *us*."

He laughs. "It was the first time I realized that you guys were my lifetime people."

"We almost..."

"We almost," he agrees. Ce la vie.

My heart lurches when he takes out the last piece. A small saucer painted with a starry sky and the moon.

"The night on the rooftop," he murmurs. "This is the history of us."

"Yeah," I answer. "It was freezing that night and I wanted to go home. You talked me into not giving up. You opened your coat and pulled me inside it and let me cry against your chest."

"I didn't want you to go. This is..." He stares at the place setting and blows out a breath. "This is better than anything I could ever give you." He's very wrong about that, because it can never compare to the soft kiss he gives me when he leans in to brush his lips against mine. "Thank you."

"You've been in every season of my life since I moved here. I don't want to have any without you. And I'm sorry for the backup plan. I was just scared that you would change your mind. It seemed like preparing for it might make it suck less? No one ever actually chooses me."

He pulls me into him and palms my cheek, looking down at me with wonder.

"No, you never let yourself be chosen." And then he says the most amazing thing. "So I may have watched Bob Ross because I was a little jealous." I smile and he swats my bottom. "Don't judge me. But he said something I can't forget. It's exactly how I feel about you. He said, 'Let's come right down in here and put some nice big strong arms on these trees. Trees need an arm too. It'll hold up the weight of the forest. Little bird has to have a place to sit there.'"

Tears burn my eyes and my throat because the simplicity and enormity of what he just said is what love is all about.

"Let me be your tree, Chloe. Let me choose you. I fucking love you with everything I have."

He loves me. Austin loves me. Every fear flies away and all the murky waters clear.

"I love you too."

His eyes flare. "Say it again."

"I love you too."

"Fuck." And then his hands are in my hair and his lips and tongue tell me this is it.

This is final. Lifetime people, like he said. We are an *us*.

Starting with the new dish named after me he serves us for dinner. He eats his off his new dishes, and tells me all about what it will say on his menu when it becomes a signature dish at his restaurant. *The Chloe* is a trofie (aka inch-long) pasta, with fresh tomatoes and herbs from our garden, a little bit of bacon ("It me!" I squeal) and a thick eight-inch sausage ("It you!" I squeal again) and just a splash of cream. I do restrain myself from adding more innuendo to that, but only because it smells too good to keep talking instead of eating.

It's amazing, and all the flavors complement each other to perfection. And then I get laid with true love.

As he slides into me, he worships my face with kisses, whispering, "I love you," over and over.

Everything from this moment on is our happily ever after.

EPILOGUE

YOU KNOW what's better than sex? Nap dates. Okay, maybe not quite as spectacular as sex, but in its category, it's pretty damn good. It's a whole event. Snuggled in a spoon with Austin is better than I could've imagined. My life is better than I could've imagined. Mae'd and Laid are doing phenomenal, Paisley is a gem, and Austin's restaurant is almost ready to officially reopen under his ownership.

"... Hey, Austin?"

"Yeah?" His groggy voice rasps against my ear as we lounge on the sofa, intertwined.

"Do you think we should get a cat? I found this awesome app called FriendsOfFur..."

"Cute. Do you give balls of string to the ones you like?"

"No, but that's genius." His hand whispers down

my side. "What's with these marketing departments? They had one job."

"Did you know I love you?" he says.

"I did know that," I say. "But I love you more."

We're so cheesy, but I don't care. I like cheese. My family loves him and so do I. When I reach over to the coffee table for my phone to show him the site, it rings.

"Chloe," James says when I answer, "help."

Charlotte wails in the background, drowning out the rest of what he says. I catch *baby* and *flood of water* and *it's time*.

"James, repeat that."

He does and it is, it appears, time for us to have this baby. And then Charlotte confirms it.

"Chloe," she pants into the phone, "meet us at the hospital. James has fainted twice and I need a backup husband to get through this birth. Also, these contractions hurt like a motherfuc—" She lets out another wail and James returns to the line.

"Have you left yet? I hope you've left."

"Be right there."

I leap from the couch and race to grab my handbag. "Get up. Nap time is over," I say to Austin. "It's baby time."

"What? Shit. Damn. Fuck. Okay, remain calm," he says, bounding from his reclined position and patting his pockets extremely un-calmly. "Where are my keys?" He holds up a hand, darting his gaze about the room. "Don't panic. Everything is going to be okay. They're here somewhere."

"I'll drive," I say, when he can't produce his keys within seconds. "Let's go before she pushes and little he or she pops out and we are not there to see it happen and welcome their baby into the world."

"Just remain calm. We need to be calm."

"I am calm," I say as we rush out the door and to my car. "You don't seem calm, though. You look pale with a tint of green. Take a deep breath. Can't have you fainting on me."

"Pfft," he says, taking the keys from me so he can drive us to the birthing center. "I'll have you know, I have a stomach of steel. I'm not a fainter and later I'm going to tie you to the bed and spank you for saying that."

His white knuckling the steering wheel says otherwise but I let him have his moment of masculinity because it's sweet he's as panicked as I am. Plus, yum to my punishment.

"We're going to be Aunt and Uncle," I say as he drives toward the hospital. "Can you believe it?"

"No," he says. "No, I can't believe any of it. We're probably going to see some blood and stretching of body parts that shouldn't stretch that far but remain calm." Streetlights illuminate the interior of the car and he's white as a ghost. "What's the speed limit? Can you go faster? Not that fast. Remain calm," he says again. "Take some deep breaths. Like this."

I side-eye his demonstration because clearly he is on the verge of an anxiety attack but I play along, because honestly, I am worried. Seeing Charlotte in pain isn't something I'm sure I can handle. The birthing center allows us to be in there with her but what if I freak out? My only experience with birth was a single video in health class freshman year. It was shocking, and I imagine many teenage pregnancies were prevented as a result.

Within twenty minutes, we are hustling down the fluorescent-lit hall toward Charlotte's private room.

"Thank God you're here," her mom says. "She's at seven centimeters so it shouldn't be much longer."

I cross to a sweaty Charlotte who is hooked up to all kinds of machines. In a hospital gown. The baby's heartbeat thumps into the room. "You aren't naked!"

"Why would I be naked?"

"The lady in my health-class video... never mind. How are you?" I ask, dropping a kiss to her forehead.

"Good," she says. "Scared but good. Hurts a little more than I expected."

Austin steps up beside me and runs a hand down my back. "You're going to be parents soon. Remain calm, even though you're certainly terrified."

A contraction causes a grimace and a long wail. James looks unsettled and Austin quickly steps to his side for moral support. An hour passes and every time Charlotte contracts, I feel it in my bones.

And then it's time. There is a flurry of activity as Charlotte prepares to push. With her moms on one side and me on the other, and James and Austin wisely choosing to stand at the head of the bed to prevent fainting in the arrival zone, we work as a team to coach her through the pushing. She squeezes our hands and her eyes, James whispering encouragement in her ear as the nurse counts for her.

I've never seen anything as beautiful as Charlotte giving life to another human. Until the baby arrives.

"It's a girl," the doctor says. "Seven pounds, eight ounces."

"A girl," I whisper, unable to stop the tears from flowing when I hear her first cry. "You have a girl."

While they clean her up, Austin, color restored, wraps me in a hug, kissing the top of my head. "That was... I have no words."

They place the most beautiful baby I've ever seen on Charlotte's chest. Gah. She's perfect. Charlotte kisses the top of her head.

"What's her name, Mama?" I ask.

"Well, we love you both so much, and we wanted to honor you, so we're naming the baby Chlaustin."

"You're...*Twilight*-ing?" I ask in horror.

"You cannot be serious," Austin says, even more horrified. "That poor child."

James cracks up. "Good grief, no, we are not serious. Meet Everly."

I trail my finger along her soft skin and whisper, "I can't wait to be your aunt." When I glance up, Austin's looking at me with major intensity. "I think I'm ready to talk about that cat," he says. "Maybe a couple of kittens."

What's next for Kayti McGee and Laurelin Paige? Who knows! We are those kind of gals who don't really keep a schedule. Sign up for Laurelin Paige's newsletter to find out what's next because Kayti isn't responsible enough to send one on her own.

PAIGE PRESS

Paige Press isn't just Laurelin Paige anymore...

Laurelin Paige has expanded her publishing company to bring readers even more hot romances.

Sign up for our newsletter to get the latest news about our releases and receive a free book from one of our amazing authors:

Laurelin Paige
Stella Gray
CD Reiss
Jenna Scott
Raven Jayne
JD Hawkins

Poppy Dunne
Lia Hunt

ALSO BY LAURELIN PAIGE

Visit my website for a more detailed reading order.

Dating Season

Bundle 1 (Spring Fling & Summer Rebound) | Bundle 2 (Fall Hard & Winter Bloom) | Bundle 3 (Spring Fever & Summer Lovin)

Also written with Kayti McGee under the name Laurelin McGee

Miss Match | Love Struck | MisTaken | Holiday for Hire

The Dirty Universe

Dirty Filthy Rich Boys - READ FREE

Dirty Duet (Donovan Kincaid)

Dirty Filthy Rich Men | Dirty Filthy Rich Love

Dirty Games Duet (Weston King)

Dirty Sexy Player | Dirty Sexy Games

Dirty Sweet Duet (Dylan Locke)

Sweet Liar | Sweet Fate

(Nate Sinclair) Dirty Filthy Fix (a spinoff novella)

Dirty Wild Trilogy (Cade Warren)

Wild Rebel | Wild War | Wild Heart

Man in Charge Duet

Man in Charge

Man in Love

Man for Me (a spinoff novella)

The Fixed Universe

Fixed Series (Hudson & Alayna)

Fixed on You | Found in You | Forever with You | Hudson | Fixed Forever

Found Duet (Gwen & JC) Free Me | Find Me

(Chandler & Genevieve) Chandler (a spinoff novella)

(Norma & Boyd) Falling Under You (a spinoff novella)

(Nate & Trish) Dirty Filthy Fix (a spinoff novella)

Slay Series (Celia & Edward)

Rivalry | Ruin | Revenge | Rising

(Gwen & JC) The Open Door (a spinoff novella)

(Camilla & Hendrix) Slash (a spinoff novella)

First and Last

First Touch | Last Kiss

Hollywood Standalones

One More Time

Close

Sex Symbol

Star Struck

Written with Sierra Simone

Porn Star | Hot Cop

ALSO BY KAYTI MCGEE

Dating Season

Bundle 1 (Spring Fling & Summer Rebound) | Bundle 2 (Fall Hard & Winter Bloom) | Bundle 3 (Spring Fever & Summer Lovin)

Written with M. Pierce

By Any Other Name

Written with Laurelin Paige as Laurelin McGee

Holiday for Hire

Miss Match

Love Struck

MisTaken: A Novella

Under the Covers novels

UnderCovers

Topped

Long Shot

Hands Off

Standalone

Screwmates

That Thing You Do

ABOUT LAURELIN PAIGE

With millions of books sold, Laurelin Paige is the NY Times, Wall Street Journal, and USA Today Bestselling Author of the Fixed Trilogy. She's a sucker for a good romance and gets giddy anytime there's kissing, much to the embarrassment of her three daughters. Her husband doesn't seem to complain, however. When she isn't reading or writing sexy stories, she's probably singing, watching shows like Killing Eve, Letterkenny, and Discovery of Witches, or dreaming of Michael Fassbender. She's also a proud member of Mensa International though she doesn't do anything with the organization except use it as material for her bio.

www.laurelinpaige.com
laurelinpaigeauthor@gmail.com

ABOUT KAYTI MCGEE

Kayti McGee is livin' deliciously in beautiful Kansas City, Missouri. Go Royals!

She also writes as the latter half of Laurelin McGee. Like her co-author Laurelin Paige, she joined Mensa for no other reason than to make their bios more interesting. Sometimes they podcast as IRL.

Stalk away at:
www.kaytimcgee.com
KaytiMcGee@gmail.com

Ingram Content Group UK Ltd.
Milton Keynes UK
UKHW041255170723
425278UK00001B/14